THE STAR STALLION

"There he is!" Richard breathed triumphantly, holding the lantern up to illuminate quite the shiniest, sleekest chestnut stallion that Harriet had ever seen. The horse sidestepped around within the narrow confines of the stall, affording her an even better view.

Harriet's gaze moved eagerly over its sleek, muscular body to the white stockings of its forelegs.

"He—he's perfect, Richard—he is," she said.

But what Harriet could not say, dared not say, was that her fellow owner of this magnificent animal, her long-ago childhood companion, her splendidly handsome and dazzlingly sophisticated step-cousin Lord Richard Stanton, was perfect as well—perfect for her. . . .

Anita Mills lives in Kansas City, Missouri, with her husband, four children, and seven cats in a restored turn-of-the-century house. A former English and history teacher, she has turned a lifelong passion for both into a writing career.

Newmarket Match

Anita Mills

A SIGNET BOOK

NEW AMERICAN LIBRARY

A DIVISION OF PENGUIN BOOKS USA INC.

SIGNET TRADEMARK REG. U.S.PAT. OFF. AND FOREIGN COUNTRIES
REGISTERED TRADEMARK—MARCA RREGISTRADA
HECHO EN DRESDEN, TN., U.S.A.

SIGNET, SIGNET CLASSIC, MENTOR, ONYX, PLUME,
MERIDIAN and NAL BOOKS are published by New American
Library, a division of Penguin Books USA Inc.,
1633 Broadway, New York, New York 10019

First Printing, October, 1989

1 2 3 4 5 6 7 8 9

PRINTED IN THE UNITED STATES OF AMERICA

1 "No! A racehorse! Bah! My only regret, Richard, is that in another two months I shall no longer be able to control your wild starts!"

"Another two months is too late!"

The young woman in the library shifted the kitten on her lap and turned a page in the book she was attempting to read. But her attention was caught by the argument coming from her father's study, and she could not help straining to hear more of it. That it was her step-cousin Richard, Viscount Sherborne, made her even more curious, for despite the restraints put on his purse by the trustees of his fortune, he lived the fashionable life of her dreams. Yes, Richard Standen was a veritable Corinthian by anyone's standards, and within a short space of time he was going to be an extremely wealthy one. Moreover, he was quite her favorite relative, blood or otherwise.

But her clutch-fisted father was not going to part with so much as a farthing over Richard's stipulated allowance, was not going to relinquish even the slightest control of the Standen fortune a day before the terms of Henry Standen's will forced him to do so. And Richard ought to have known he wasted his breath in arguing the point.

"But it isn't just any racehorse, Uncle," she heard

5

her step-cousin explain. " 'Tis a natural, I tell you! I have seen it run, and there's none to compare for power and grace! 'Tis a certain winner!"

"Humph! It's in the blood, I suppose," her father snorted. "Aye, if your father'd not been hell-born himself and broken his neck for a stupid wager before he was ruined, I doubt he'd have left you a tuppence to squander! There it is—I've said it! You are no less a scapegrace than he was!"

"It's my money, Uncle," Richard reminded him evenly, his voice dropping with what she could only consider admirable restraint.

"Not for another two months!"

Harriet Rowe could see in her mind how his jaw must be working to hold what he could of his Standen temper. Completely cuaght up in the contretemps in the study, she closed the book and leaned forward, stroking the sleeping kitten absently. Surely Richard must know there was no budging her father—how well she could tell him that.

"I could make a bloody fortune with that horse, Uncle John," the younger man pleaded. "You have not seen it—at least come look before you deny me."

"My mind is set, I tell you! The answer is no! And when all's said and done—when your salad days are behind you—you will thank me for it," Sir John sniffed sanctimoniously.

In her chair, Harriet mouthed the words even as he said them, for she'd had years of listening to just such lectures. Indeed, she'd been treated to one but yesterday when she'd timidly ventured to suggest that she leave the misery of his house to set up a quiet establishment with her old nurse, Miss Violet Plimly, and Plimly's elderly sister Agnes in Bath.

"Bath!" he'd howled, as though Bath were some hotbed of license and indecency. "No, missy, you will not! If you were fool enough to remain unwed, you are scarce fit to fend for yourself out in the world! How should it appear before the world, I ask you, if 'twere known you had left your father's protection? No, missy—'twill not serve!"

And not even the reminder that she had her own competency had moved him. Quite the contrary, in fact, for it brought home to him again that her late mother had been remiss by allowing a female child an inheritance ungoverned by her father or any other responsible male upon her majority.

"As to that, missy, I can only say I'll not allow you to waste your competence! An establishment of your own! No! Rather than thinking of such a thing, you should be asking my advice about investing in the funds!" And then he'd ended with his usual lecture. "Aye, when you are naught but an aged spinster in this house, you will thank me for the care I have given you, Harriet, though I must admit 'tis a sorrow to me that you have set yourself against the married state. Hannah cannot quite like it, you know—two grown females in the same household is like oil and water, after all, and they do not set well together."

The care he had given her. 'Twas a jest at best, she thought rebelliously. All he'd done after her mother's death was to remarry a widow as cold as he was, and between them they'd made it plain from the very beginning that a female child was naught but a burden. They'd put no expense into a Season for her, Hannah sniffing 'twould be but money wasted, for Harriet was too shy to take. And it was true, Harriet supposed, for the thought of parading about on the Marriage Mart had terrified her. But they'd expected her to take the vicar's second son, a singularly pompous, stolid man who positively hated cats. And when she'd refused his suit, they'd punished her in a dozen ways, making it plain they begrudged her very presence, calling her naught but a spinster repeatedly, and yet denying her any escape but marriage. It was no wonder that her only brother had bought a commission and fled from the dreary life at Rowe's Hill.

The door to her father's study opened, and she could hear her step-cousin gathering his hat and stick from a footman. Impulsively she dumped the kitten gently to the floor and slipped out into the hall as he disappeared out the front door. She raced for the back door and sped around the house, holding her skirts decorously above her slippers.

"Psssst! Richard!" she hissed from around the corner.

He'd been about to mount the step of his curricle when he heard her. He hesitated, his face betraying his anger and his impatience. Clearly he was in no mood for the merest pleasantry with anyone.

"Over here!" She tried to keep her voice low enough not to draw her father's attention.

Richard turned around, ready to give whoever it was a sharp set-down, and then he saw her. And for once there was a certain mischief in those dark eyes of hers that reminded him of another time, a time when they'd been children together, shortly after his aunt's marriage to her father. She'd been a lively girl once, but that was before years of his Aunt Hannah's sober strictures and cold dislike had taken their toll. Now she'd become a quiet, timid woman, one who'd failed in the expected quest of a husband. And at twenty-four she was but a spinster on the proverbial shelf, doomed to remain in her father's house under his Aunt Hannah's dominance. He felt a surge of pity for her, and yet he could not entirely forget his anger.

"What is it, Harry? I've scarce got time—" Her

face fell, and he relented. "All right. I suppose I am not in such a hurry as all that."

"Shhhhhh." She beckoned to him from the corner of the house. "I heard the quarrel with my father, Richard," she told him as he came closer. "I could not help it."

"I'll wager the whole household did," he muttered dryly.

"Is it truly a wonderful horse?"

He was about to retort that it didn't make any difference now, that it was going to be someone else's horse anyway, but there was an eagerness, an almost childlike intensity in those dark, appealing eyes. "Yes," he answered simply. "Yes, it is."

"What color is it?"

"What difference does that make?" he snapped, his irritation returning. "Color doesn't have anything to do with how well a horse runs, Harry."

"I just wanted to know if it were pretty."

The wistfulness in her voice was unmistakable. Reminding himself that it was not her fault her father was so obstinate, he unbent again. "It's a chestnut—and yes, it's a very handsome animal. Does that satisfy you?" he asked more gently.

"And you are certain it can run—can compete, I mean?"

"Harry, with a little training, this horse could win at Newmarket—or anywhere. He's a two-year-old thoroughbred—a direct descendant of the Godolphin Barb." He walked around the house, drawing her out of view of anyone else, warming to the subject of the horse he wanted desperately. " 'Tis difficult to believe, I know, but the man who owns him is quite elderly and has no interest in racing him."

"But if 'tis such a wonderful animal, why does

he offer it to you?" she questioned reasonably. "You have not the least experience with a racehorse, have you?"

"No, Harry, I do not, but 'tis unimportant—there are trainers for that sort of thing. Hawleigh has some affection for me—he's an old bachelor with no close heirs. Anyway, I have listened to his stories for years, out of politeness mostly, but I guess he did not see it quite that way. Then when I saw this colt of his and thought it had prospects, I made mention of it to him, and he told me then I should have the first opportunity should he decide to sell."

"And now he wishes to sell it?"

"His health fails him, and he has not the inclination anymore."

"I see."

"No, you cannot, I fear." He sighed, recalling again the horse he wanted so badly. "Well, now that 'tis old enough to race as a colt this year, I *know* 'tis the best animal I have ever been privileged to see. It has the speed of the wind, Harry, and the old man doesn't wish the bother of racing him."

"I see," she murmured again, looking up at her handsome step-cousin, taking in the rakish set of his hat, the slight curl ofh is black hair around his face, his bright blue eyes, his strong, straight features, the faint curve of his mouth. Richard Standen had been the ideal of her youth, the one who dared do things she only dreamed of.

"Anything else, Harry?" he asked, eager to leave Rowe's Hill and his uncle's ignominious refusal behind him.

"Yes." She cleared her throat nervously, her heart thudding at the daring thought that came to mind. "How much does the horse cost?"

"What difference does it make?" He sighed heavily again, looking away, squinting his eyes against the winter sun. "My pockets are let to quarter day, and there's another buyer. If Uncle William had not died last year, I daresay he'd have let me have my money, but now that your father is the only trustee . . . I should have sold something, but now 'tis too late. Old Hawleigh wanted to give me the first chance, that's all—he knows I'd take care of his horse and not push the animal too hard and ruin it."

"But how much would it take—to buy it, I mean?" she persisted.

"That's the thing of it, Harry. Hawleigh would have let me have him for only a thousand pounds. For any other, 'tis more than twice that much."

A thousand pounds. She gulped at the seeming enormity of the sum. "One thous . . . *one thousand pounds*, Richard?"

"I know, it sounds like a lot, but a good racehorse is worth a lot more than that. The stud fees alone can reach three hundred fifty pounds once he's retired. And that's not counting the purses—in a single season, a horse can run at Newmarket, Doncaster, Epsom, and a lot of the smaller tracks— not to mention on the Continent."

"I see." Her mind racing with her heart now, she moved in front of him and reached to touch one of the layered capes of his greatcoat where it hung over his arm. "Then a horse would be an investment, wouldn't it?"

"I wish Uncle John could see it as clearly as that. Yes, a horse like that would be an excellent investment, Harry. 'Tis what I was trying to tell him. And it wasn't as though I wanted *him* to buy it," he muttered with feeling. "I did but ask for what is going to be mine in a matter of weeks anyway, you know."

One thousand pounds. Harriet sucked in her

breath and let it out in a rush, both afraid and exhilarated by what she meant to do. "I should like to invest in your horse, Richard," she managed, her fingers tightening convulsively on the heavy woolen cloth, tugging it.

At first he didn't think he'd heard her right, but as he stared down into her upturned face, he realized she was indeed serious. "*You*, Harry?"

"Well, why not?" The words, once they came, tumbled out excitedly. "Papa is always urging me to invest the competence Mama left me, and—"

"I couldn't take your money," he cut in gently. "I'd not ask it of you."

"But if you think the horse is going to be a winner—"

"I wouldn't feel right about it, Harry. Things can happen—even to the best plans. I wouldn't want to risk your money."

"Fiddle. I want to do it." Her dark eyes met his, sobering, and she nodded. "You don't understand—I *want* to do it. I never do anything the least extraordinary, Richard, and I think owning a racehorse would be wonderful."

"No. You cannot have that much to risk."

"I have exactly two thousand pounds, so I shall not be destitute anyway, and besides, I should expect you to pay half of it back when you come into your inheritance. And I should expect to share in your winnings, after all."

"Uncle John—"

"My father doesn ot control my inheritance, Richard. I think Mama realized how it would be before she died. I had my brother place it in a bank in London before he left."

"George—"

"No. Not my brother either. When I reached twenty-one, I gained full disposal of it."

He looked down, taking in the plain knot of brown hair at the nape of her neck, the almost shapeless blue gown she wore, and he resolutely backed away. "You should spend your money on yourself, Harry."

"As if I ever go anywhere or do anything!" she snorted in disgust. "No, my mind is quite made up, I think—I should like to own at least half of a race-horse."

Later, he was to blame it on the temptation of the horse, but just then he read the eagerness, the spirit, the enthusiasm shining in those dark eyes, something he had not seen in a number of years, and he could not refuse her offer.

"I'll pay all of it back, Harry."

"I told you—I wish to be a partner in the venture, Richard. You pay me five hundred pounds and half of anything the horse wins."

An impish, delighted smile spread over her usually somber face, reassuring him that she did indeed want to lend him the money. He held out his hand as he would have to another man, and she took it. "Then partners we are, Harry. But if you ever decide you wish to cash in, you have but to tell me, and I will repay you every pound, I promise you."

"No. It is enough to share an adventure with you. And besides"—the dimples at the corners of her mouth deepened—"it is just possible that your horse will make me rich, isn't it?"

Her smile was infectious. His humor restored completely, he grinned back at her. "And if he does not?"

"He will—I know it."

Still holding her hand, Richard leaned over and brushed a brotherly kiss against her cheek. "You know, Harry, I always did think you were a very good sort of a girl."

"What fustian!" she retorted, blushing to the roots of her soft brown hair. "You teased me unmercifully—and you know it. And you were forever getting me into your scrapes, too." She pulled her hand away and stepped back self-consciously. "Yes, well . . . I shall give you a draft on my bank in London, if 'tis settled. And then you'd best be going before Papa suspects what I have done."

2 Harriet drew her legs up under her skirts and held Richard's letter closer to the faint winter's light coming through the windowpane. Two Harry? She stopped and read the line again— he'd named their horse Two Harry, he said, to reflect their joint ownership. Two Harry for Harriet Rowe and Richard Henry Thomas Standen. She chuckled, delighted by that small recognition of her contribution, and wondered if the name would give her away. No, she decided, casting a surreptitious look at her father as he read his paper across the room. No, he lacked the imagination to ever see any connection.

Sir John Rowe looked up and frowned. "If you must display your unseemly levity, I would that you went somewhere else, Harriet."

"Well, I for one cannot think what my nephew could possibly want to write to her," Hannah Rowe murmured as she continued to stitch along the border of a table runner.

"Your nevvy? Here now, miss, I'll not have you setting your cap for the likes of Sherborne—you hear me? The Standens may be plump in the pocket, but they're a havey-cavey bunch. Besides, stands to reason he'd want better'n a baron's daughter, anyway."

15

"Papa!"

"Humph! As if she'd have the chance!" Hannah sniffed. "With his looks and fortune, he can expect an Incomparable."

"And if half the stories I've heard are true, he'll be in dun territory within a year! Rich as Croesus, but the blood's bad!" He cast a quick look at his wife's stiffening expression and hastened to add, "Not on your side, my dear—'twas the Standens I meant." Then he turned his full attention on his daughter, demanding sternly, "Just what does Sherborne write?"

Caught by her father's bushy-browed stare, Harriet cast about wildly in her mind for a plausible explanation, particularly since Richard was not in the habit of writing to her. At that moment the kitten in her lap reached playfully to bat at the paper she held. She looked down.

"Oh . . . uh . . . a kitten."

Hannah Rowe's eyebrow rose skeptically as she eyed her stepdaughter curiously. "What?"

"That is, he would like to have a kitten."

"Nonsense! 'Tis plain as a pikestaff, Harriet, that you have inherited your own mama's silliness," Sir John complained. "A cat indeed!"

"If Richard writes that he wants a cat, it must surely be his notion of a jest."

Thus attacked, Harriet felt compelled to stand her ground, however tenuous it might be. "Oh, no—he does."

"Do you mean to tell me that Sherborne is actually asking for a *cat*? I cannot credit it, missy! What queer start is this?"

For a moment Harriet feared he was going to demand to read Richard's letter for himself, but then Hannah nodded. "Well, I suppose that does explain it, after all—I knew he could not be attempting to fix his interest with her."

"No, of course not," Harriet agreed quickly. "If you will excuse me, I will write back that Athena had but two and therefore a kitten is out of the question."

"You'll do no such thing, miss! If Sherborne wants a cat he can have the lot of 'em! I have never liked 'em anyway! Dashed nuisances, always rubbing against a man's leg, tripping him. Can't think why a man like Sherborne would want one— I'd expect him to prefer a good hound. Cats is for silly females!"

She made good her escape, and lying on her bed within the safety of her room, she reread Richard's entire letter. He'd had no difficulty cashing her draft, he told her, and he'd bought the horse almost beneath Lord Elmore's nose, despite his rival's offer of considerably more money. A bargain was a bargain, Hawleigh had insisted, honoring his arrangement with Richard. And then there was the explanation about the name. "It has occasioned more than a little comment," he wrote, "for few know I bear the name Henry also, and everyone is casting about in search of its source. When I registered the change in the General Stud Book, I overheard Siddells speculate at the Jockey Club that 'twas in honor of my father and grandfather, actually."

The small kitten jumped up on the bed beside her and stood on its hind legs to claw at the paper in her hand. "Not now, Abelard." She scooped him up and nuzzled him, rubbing her cheek against the long black fur. "You know," she mused aloud to the squirming creature, "I wish 'twere possible to see this horse I have bought. But," she sighed regretfully, "Papa would never hear of it. Indeed, he must never know what I have done, else he will be unbearable."

The kitten stopped wriggling and tucked its head under her chin, purring loudly. That was perhaps what she liked best about animals—they loved without judging, returning full measure the care she lavished on them.

Footsteps sounded in the hall, slowing to a stop outside her door. She sat up hastily and crumpled Sherborne's letter into a ball before throwing it into the fire that burned in the small fireplace. It caught immediately, flaring briefly and sending bits of paper ash into the air.

"Well, miss, what nonsense is this?" Hannah Rowe demanded, stepping into the room. "A fire?" She sniffed. "How many times have I told you that when there's fires downstairs, you will be pleased to sit at them and not waste wood foolishly?"

"Frequently," Harriet muttered.

"What?"

"I said I am sorry for it."

"Yes, well, and you should be. Bedchambers are for sleeping rather than sitting, anyway."

Then she caught sight of the kitten and her frown deepened. "I thought I'd made it plain that you are not to keep animals in your room. I consider it unhealthy." She moved closer, reaching for the black kitten. "Animals," she pronounced firmly, "belong outside."

" 'Tis too cold and he is small," Harriet protested, holding Abelard closer.

"Nonsense. 'Tis why God gave such things fur. Really, Harriet, but you are absurd in the extreme. One would think you prefer the dirty little things over your fellowman, if the truth were known."

"Mayhap I find them kinder."

"What a queer creature you are, to be sure. But then, I have never understood how it is that you have no wish for an establishment of your own."

"Surely Papa must have told you that—"

"That nonsense about Bath?" The older woman's eyebrows rose disdainfully. "My dear Harriet, it cannot be done—people would say that your papa was remiss if he allowed such a thing, and well you know it. Miss Plimly, however unexceptional she may be, is simply not of your class. No—I was referring to dear Mr. Thornton." She stepped back, dropping her hand as Abelard hissed at her, and drew close to warm herself at the fire. Her mouth stretched into a thin smile as she turned again to her stepdaughter, and her voice became only slightly more conciliatory. "All is not lost in that quarter, you know. Only yesterday Mr. Thornton was asking your papa about you, and—"

"I have no wish to fix my interest with Mr. Thornton," Harriet cut in tiredly. "We should not suit."

"If you would but try, I am sure—"

"I do not wish to try."

"Every female must want a husband . . . a home . . . children to call her own, Harriet, and Mr. Thornton—"

"But I don't *like* Edwin Thornton."

"And that is nothing to the point," Hannah retorted in exasperation. "Passion is vastly overrated when it comes to actually living with a husband. While it may serve in those foolish novels you read—and do not think I do not know what it is that you order on subscription, for I do—anyway, as I was saying, you will find that a comfortable income is much more important than one's feelings in the matter. And Mr. Thornton is reasonably well-circumstanced, after all. There, I have said it. Now—"

"I find Edwin Thornton to be overbearing, pompous, and dull, Mama. There, I have said that, Mama." She looked up quickly to see the effect of that pronouncement, and then hastily looked down for fear Hannah would seek to punish her for her insolence.

"Your papa has given him leave to pay calls on you again, Harriet, and it is to be hoped this time that you are not so foolish. A twenty-four-year-old spinster cannot afford to be so—"

"Difficult to please?" Goaded by this unpleasant bit of news, Harriet risked defying her stepmama openly. "Alas, but I am, I fear. I'd far rather remain unwed all the days of my life, Mama, then take Mr. Thornton merely because he is the only man to offer for me."

The smile vanished from Hannah Rowe's face, replaced by a look bordering on dyspepsia. "Foolish girl! You cannot wish to hang on your papa's purse forever! 'Tis time and past time that you were gone from this house, missy!"

"Then persuade Papa to let me live with Plimly and I will gladly go! As for hanging on Papa's purse, there's precious little of that I have seen!" Harriet's eyes flashed now, betraying a rare spark of rebellion. "Look at this room, Mama—and look at my clothes! All I have is bought with my own mama's portion!"

"Of all the ungrateful . . . the . . ." Words failed Lady Rowe for a moment, and then, before Harriet realized her intent, she snatched the kitten from Harriet's shoulder. "I have tolerated you and these filthy little beasts far too long in my house! Aye, and your insolent tongue also!"

Carrying the frightened, clawing kitten as though it were a snake, Hannah marched from the room, slamming the door. Harriet stared after her with growing consternation, knowing she'd exceeded the bounds of what was acceptable to her stepmama. And years of living in the same household had taught her that Hannah's retribution was swift and stern.

"Wait! Mama, wait!" She hurried down the hall after her, suddenly afraid again. "I did not mean—"

"John! John!"

Harriet's father emerged from the front saloon, his paper still in his hand, as Hannah reached the bottom stair. And one look told him that his wife was angered with his daughter yet again. Before he could retreat to whence he had come, Hannah thrust the indignantly writhing kitten at him.

"You will drown the beast! I'll not tolerate another cat in this house! Thomas! Thomas!"

"My lady?" The lower footman appeared from the back serving hall promptly.

"You will discover the mother cat and the other kitten immediately, and you will drown them!"

"I say . . ." Sir John protested feebly. "It's dashed cold out, and—"

"Mama!" Harriet screeched.

"John!" Hannah reproached her husband.

He looked from one woman to the other and then back to the black kitten that clung to his coat. "Well, perhaps the stables or the—"

"John!"

"Yes, well, but—"

"Papa, I will keep them out of her way—I swear it!" Harriet pleaded, fighting against tears.

"Here, missy! How is it that you and your mama are always at daggers drawn, anyway? Seems to me . . ."

Harriet wanted to shout that Hannah Belford Rowe was not her mama, but she bit her tongue and tried to conciliate instead. Hanging her head, she murmured, "I suppose the fault was mine, Papa, but I had no wish to entertain Mr. Thornton's suit."

"Thornton's suit? What in the deuce does that have to do with drowning cats, I ask you? And as for Thornton, you most certainly shall be all that is pleasant to him—I expect it! And when he dines here tonight, you will wear your best gown!"

"Yes, Papa," she managed meekly, hiding the impotent rage and terror that warred within her heart. If she'd learned naught else in Hannah's house, she knew tears were a weakness that availed her nothing. "If you will not harm the cats, I will be all that is polite to Mr. Thornton."

"No, missy—'tis too late for such a mealy mouth now," Hannah told her maliciously. "My mind is set—I'll not have cats in my house!" Turning to her husband, she added firmly, "I shall expect you to get rid of them."

"Papa, please!"

"Well, now . . ."

"John!"

"I suppose they could go to the barn," he ventured, looking down on the huddling kitten.

"I want them drowned today." Casting a triumphant glance at Harriet, Hannah added smugly, "As for you, missy, you may stay in your room until dinner and consider your manners to me."

It didn't matter then. Harriet gazed lovingly at the black kitten, her dark eyes bright and brimming. "Papa, if you kill an innocent creature at her whim, I will refuse to even so much as speak to Mr. Thornton," she managed in a low whisper, despite the tight ache in her chest.

Sir John was in the position he liked least, caught between his wife and his daughter. For once, he did not immediately do Hannah's bidding. Instead, he shook his head irritably and put them both off.

"We'll see—after I have finished my paper."

"There's no room in one household for two mistresses, John," Hannah warned direly, and then she turned on her heel, stalking stiffly toward the back of the house.

"You'd best get to your room, Harriet. I won't live with my house at sixes and sevens between you, you hear me?"

"Say you'll not kill them, Papa."

"Can you not conciliate her? Must you always set yourself against her?" he demanded rhetorically. "No, I suppose you cannot."

"Papa . . ." She wanted to shout that she'd tried, that she'd sought to please Hannah since she was but a small child, but that Hannah could not be pleased. Instead, her protest died on her lips. If she forced the matter now, she knew she'd lose her cats forever.

"Humph! We'll see. As for you, missy, I'll expect you to be more than merely civil to young Thornton, you hear? Aye, and I'd have you wear something decent this time! And for God's sake, do something with that hair! I won't have him thinking you are even older than you are!"

Having won a brief reprieve for her animals, Harriet fled to the haven of her room, throwing herself on her bed. She was four-and-twenty, and yet she might as well have been a small naughty child, the way they treated her. And she had no illusions that it would ever change, because Hannah would never be satisfied until she'd rid herself of an unwanted stepdaughter.

The cats were but one more pain to be borne, and

Harriet had reached the point where she could no longer bear it. For a moment she even considered Edwin Thornton, but she knew in her heart that she'd be just as miserable as his wife—marrying Edwin would be like marrying a male Hannah. Tears of self-pity, too long stifled, rolled down her cheeks unchecked as she drew her coverlet about her and tried to keep warm. She was so enveloped in her own misery that she didn't even hear the commotion in the lower hall.

Sir John had been about to dispose of Abelard into Thomas' arms with the admonition to take him to the stables and keep him out of sight when the sounds of a carriage rolling down the drive brought him up short. He peered out the tall, small-paned windows that framed the double front doors, wondering who would brave the cold for a visit. The black lacquered coach pulled up almost to the steps, disgorging none other than Sherborne himself. Under other circumstances, Sir John would have been less than pleased to see his wife's scapegrace nephew, but in this case he was relieved.

A gust of cold wind blew in as the door was opened to admit the viscount. And with a crow of triumph Sir John thrust the kitten at him as Richard handed his caped greatcoat to the footman.

"Here—'tis yours, sirrah, though what you can want with the beast, I am sure I don't know. A man with a cat—humph! And while you are about it, you might as well have the mother and the other one too! Saves me the trouble of having 'em drowned and listening to Harriet weep over it!"

With that, he strode off, paper still in hand, toward the warmth of the front saloon. For a long moment Richard stared after him, thinking his uncle had lost his mind. And then he looked down at the fuzzy black ball that both chewed and clawed at the leather of his fine driving glove.

"Er . . . Thomas, is it? Would you be so kind as to inform Miss Rowe that I am here?" he addressed the footman, still bemused by the creature straddling his wrist. "And ask her to hurry—I am not overly fond of cats."

3 By the time Harriet got downstairs, Richard Standen was engaged in gingerly disentangling his glove from Abelard's teeth and claws. Grinning ruefully, he looked up as she rounded the first landing.

"There you are, Harry. Do you think you could possibly retrieve this beast before he ruins ten pounds?"

"Ten pounds? How can that be?" she asked with a faint lift to an eyebrow. "Surely you cannot have spent that much on a pair of gloves."

But as she came off the last step, he could see the twitch at the corners of her mouth as she tried hard not to laugh. "I fail to see what amuses you," he muttered with feeling. "I had scarce crossed the threshold when this animal was literally thrown onto my arm, Harry. Ouch, you little devil!" He paused to remove his blue superfine coat sleeve from the kitten's teeth, but Abelard had now managed to cling to his forearm from beneath, hanging firmly by all four feet. "I didn't wish to harm it, of course, but I am less than fond of cats—even yours," he complained. "Otherwise, I should have thrown it to the floor."

Unsympathetic to his plight, Harriet failed to suppress her laughter and dissolved into an outright giggle. Her dark eyes sparkling, she reached

26

for Abelard. "Oh, Richard, I never thought I should see it—Richard Standen treed by a cat, of all things, and a helpless k-kitten at that!" Her slender fingers gently lifted the black furball from the coat sleeve, disengaging its small claws carefully. "Oh, dear, some of the threads are quite pulled, I fear."

"Thank you. And I was not 'treed,' precisely," he retorted. "I told you—I didn't want to hurt it or the coat. But I take leave to tell you that I think your father is more than a trifle touched in his upper works these days, Harry," he fumed. "He dropped that thing on me and then just walked off, saying something about my wanting cats."

"Oh." She flushed guiltily and dropped her head as she rubbed the fluffy fur behind the kitten's ears. Her voice regretful, her face averted, she admitted, "Yes . . . well, I fear some of the fault is mine, you see." Then, daring to meet his blue eyes, she plunged into an explanation. "Well, I was afraid they would demand to see your letter, and I could think of no plausible reason why you should be writing to me, Richard, so I said you were inquiring about a cat—or, to be more precise, that you were wishful of a kitten."

"You told them I wanted a *cat*? Whatever for? Could you not have said I just wanted to write a letter to you? Harry—" He stopped short, noting that the animation had left her face and her eyes, and his voice dropped as he added more kindly, "Harry, you should not have to explain anything so insignificant as a letter to anyone."

"Tell Hannah that," she responded bitterly, looking away again. "You cannot know how it is to have to answer for every single thing, can you? You are a man, after all, and therefore free to do as you please, so you cannot understand. Well, I am not allowed to have my own opinions, my own friends

. . . or . . . or kittens even!" Tears welled in her eyes, brightening them, before she hastily rubbed the wetness away.

"Egad! I'd no notion, of course—I mean, I knew it could not be very comfortable for you with my aunt, but I thought . . ."

"You are a man, Richard," she repeated. "You do not have to answer to the conventions of society, to a stepmama like Hannah, or to—"

"Can you not just leave?" He caught himself, realizing she spoke the truth, that it was different for a female. "Surely Uncle John—"

A harsh, derisive, brittle laugh escaped her. "My father? You jest, of course. He takes her side in even the smallest struggles between us. If aught can be said of Sir John Rowe, sir, 'tis that he prizes peace above all things."

"I'm sorry, Harry."

She regained her composure by nuzzling the purring kitten with her cheek, and then she did the unthinkable—she sniffed. "Your pardon, my lord— 'twas not my intent to burden you with my small problems. 'Tis just that I am blue-deviled, but no matter—I shall come about."

"Harry . . . Harry . . ." He reached a comforting hand to clasp the hand that held the kitten. "I have known you since I was in short coats and you were but a scrubby little girl in a torn gown—remember that?"

Recovering, she nodded, and a faint smile curved her mouth. "Yes, and I recall that it was because of you that I tore it—I *tried* to tell you that Papa's bull was mean."

"That's better. I like it when you display at least some spirit. We are partners, after all, are we not? If there's aught that I can do to ease your circumstances, you have but to ask, you know."

She hesitated, turning her attention once again to the kitten in her arms, and then sighed. "All right—but you will not like the answer, I fear." Sucking in her breath, she raised her dark eyes to his, and it was impossible to miss the appeal in them. "Then would you be so very kind as to take my cats? Oh, I know you think you would not like having the kittens, but perhaps you could learn—I mean, if you do not say you will take them, Hannah means to have them drowned." Her voice, hesitant at first, rushed to finish her plea before he could deny what she asked. "Richard, I beg of you—do not let her kill poor innocent creatures! Say you will help me!"

He was taken aback by the urgency of her entreaty, and for a moment he was at a loss for words. "Me?" he choked finally. "Harry, I have just told you—I don't like cats!"

"Please, Richard—please," she wheedled, tears welling anew. "Even if you will do no more than take them to your hunting box or to your country home, they will at least have more of a chance than if they are put in a sack and dropped in the river. Richard—"

"Tell you what," he interrupted desperately, "I'll speak with Aunt Hannah myself, and—"

"No!" She clutched at his sleeve, her voice growing more agitated. "You still don't understand, do you? Even if she says she will let them live, 'tis but for now. You see, she knows—she *knows* now what they mean to me and she will use them whenever she is vexed. And if I do not take Mr. Thornton's offer, they will be drowned!"

"Come on, Harry—I did not come to have you enact a Cheltenham tragedy for me." Gently disengaging her fingers from his arm, he clasped her hand reassuringly. "It cannot be as bad as all that—ten to one, she will have forgotten all about the damned . . . the *deuced* cats, ere tomorrow. If you will but keep them out of her sight—"

She made one last bid. "Richard, I will consider the loan repaid if you will but do as I ask."

"No! Dash it, Harry! I'd as lief pay you a cent per cent's interest as take a cat! No, I tell you!"

She swallowed hard to fight the lump that rose in her throat, and tried to regain her dignity. "Very well then. I should not have asked it of you." Clutching the black furball close, she managed to whisper, "If you will but excuse me, I . . . I've matters to attend just now."

And before he could stop her, she'd fled up the stairs. Richard stared after her, feeling somehow guilty. "I say, Harry . . . but . . ." But she'd already turned the corner at the top of the steps and was out of hearing. He looked down at the pulled threads on his sleeve and reminded himself just how much he hated cats. And a sense of injustice stole over him; he'd traveled miles out of his way to tell her about Two Harry, and she had not bothered to ask of the horse at all.

In keeping with the parsimony of Hannah, Lady Rowe, Sir John's table was remarkable only for its limited selection. Richard Standen, seated at the opposite end from his host, surveyed the single joint of meat, the plain roast goose, and the three dishes of vegetables, and wondered why he'd bothered coming all the way to Rowe's Hill. To make matters worse, he'd still not had a chance to share his enthusiasm for Two Harry with Harriet, for she sat in low-spirited silence beside Edwin Thornton, who insisted on monopolizing the conversation, sprinkling it liberally with "my lords" whenever he addressed Richard, which was far too frequently.

Mr. Thornton, it was quickly discovered, had opinions on everything, no matter how trivial the matter might be. The weather he pronounced "abominable," the results of the Vienna Congress "regrettable," the fashionable life "sinful," the current female style of dress "shameful," and Hannah More's campaign to improve the lot of the poor "foolish and hopeless." "The poor," he maintained stoutly, "are but reaping the wages of indolence."

It was at this latter statement that Harriet showed a spark of animation. Darting a furtive look at her stepmama first, she turned back to her dinner companion.

"How can it be indolence when they have not the basic requirements of existence? I think everyone has a right to decent food, warm clothing, and a place to—"

"Harriet," Lady Rowe cut in coldly, "I am sure that neither Mr. Thornton nor Sherborne cares in the least what you think. Females should not concern themselves with that which they do not understand."

From where Richard watched, he could see his step-cousin bite her lower lip to stifle a retort, and as the young woman bent her head lower, he felt a surge of anger at his aunt. "On the contrary," he heard himself say, "I for one am always interested in what Harriet thinks. If the females in this society do not attempt to improve the lot of all of us, then I fear we shall succumb to the baser nature of man and care not at all." He was rewarded by a quick glance of pure gratitude from his step-cousin. "I believe when we discourage ladies from thinking, we rob ourselves of full half of the available intelligence in this country."

"Nonsense!" Sir John exploded. "If the females

were in charge of things, we'd be in a sorry pass,
I can tell you. Why, they're the weaker sex, sirrah!
We'd be a nation of featherbrains!"

"Weaker, Uncle?" Richard's gaze traveled significantly to where Hannah sat, her eyes now fixed
malevolently on her stepdaugther. "I have never
thought my aunt weak in the least, I am sure."

"Humph! At least she don't think she can rule
things—she don't try to reform the country."

"No, she is content enough to rule you," Harriet
muttered under her breath.

"What? What's that, you say?" her father
demanded, turning a baleful eye on her. "Speak up!
I'll not have you gainsaying me in my own house,
missy! If you've something to say, out with it!"

"It was of no consequence, Papa," she mumbled,
coloring as everyone stared at her.

"I am sure Miss Rowe meant no disrespect,"
Edwin Thornton allowed. "Indeed, I have often
thought her possessed of good but sometimes mis-
guided intentions. The firm instruction of a sensible
husband—"

"I do not want a husband." She looked up, as
though to see the effect of this open pronouncement, and then hastily averted her eyes again. "I
know 'tis perverse of me, but I prefer the single
state."

"Perverse! Of course 'tis perverse! Females are
put on this earth to marry, missy!" her father
roared.

For a moment Richard thought his uncle was
going to choke on the food in his mouth, but the
redness in his face subsided and he addressed
Thornton with a broad wave of his fork. "Pay her
no heed, sir—maidenly reserve . . . that sort of
thing. She don't mean it, do you, my dear?" There

was a significant edge to his voice this time, as though she dared not dispute it.

"Of course she did not mean it," Thornton agreed. "Indeed, I have ever thought—"

"Er, would someone pass the carrots?" Richard interrupted. "I believe I should like some more. Excellent, madam, excellent," he added to his aunt. "Quite a flavorful glaze to them."

"Well, they are but caramelized with sugar, of course, but are a favorite of dear Mr. Thornton's, I believe."

"Indeed they are," Thornton agreed readily. "I should take some more also."

Sir John, grateful to avoid any further contretemps at his table, settled back in his chair and let the matter drop. Conversation again lapsed, except for Thornton, who seemed to feel it incumbent to fill any awkward silences, and who continued expounding between mouthfuls of the approved carrots. Richard gritted his teeth, wished he had not come, and determined to leave as soon as he'd made an accounting of Two Harry's progress to Harriet.

He found himself watching her as the meal progressed, and he could not help contrasting the almost cowed young woman with the vivacious child he remembered. Whereas most shy girls grew more self-confident with age, Harriet Rowe had reversed the process, and he knew whom to blame for that. What his overbearing aunt and her ineffectual father had done to her was little short of criminal. It was no wonder she had not taken when she emerged from the schoolroom—there was too little animation left to attract any but a pompous fool like Thornton. And it was not that Harriet was unpleasant in appearance, but rather that she lacked the required beauty to compensate for her quiet shyness. To a stranger she would seem dull and plain, thereby ensuring her of little more than the most casual appraisal. She was by virtue of her unmarried state, then, a prisoner, both physically and emotionally, of her unloving family.

Her attention focused intently on her plate now, she appeared to be enduring rather than enjoying her companion's dull conversation, mumbling incomprehensible replies that somehow satisfied Thornton and yet required no real social intercourse. Her dark eyes bore a carefully schooled expression that revealed nothing. But Richard's memory could hark back to a time when they sparkled with mischief, widened with the curiosity of youth, and danced with laughter. But that was years ago—fourteen, to be precise.

She turned her head to answer a blunt question from her father, and all Richard could see then was the neat twist of brown braid pinned at the nape, a totally unfashionable style that became her not at all. But Thornton did not seem to mind. Clearly the stolid Edwin was so impressed with his own opinions that he noted not at all that Harriet Rowe did not appear to share them in the least. In fact, he had the appearance of a man trying to fix his interest, determined to discover in his chosen lady a mirror of himself.

Unfortunately, just as the covers were being removed for dessert, the unmistakable and persistent meowing of a cat desiring freedom reverberated through the house. Hannah Rowe stopped in mid-sentence, her irritation evident on her thin-lipped face.

"I was under the impression that you had disposed of that matter," she remarked, her eyes accusing her husband of dereliction in his duty.

"Ah . . . yes . . . yes, I did, my dear. Gave 'em to Sherborne, didn't I?" Sir John cast a speaking appeal at Richard.

"A cat? Whatever for?" Thornton demanded curiously. "Surely not . . . That is to say . . ." He paused, quelled by Richard's expression of open dislike, and then finished lamely, "I cannot abide the creatures myself, and cannot think that a man . . . well, a cat ain't a man's animal, after all."

Richard, who was about to deny any affinity for cats himself, noted that Harriet sat white-faced and stricken, her agitation betrayed by the twisting of her napkin in her hands. Her earlier appeal seemed to ring in his ears. *Richard, do not let her kill poor innocent creatures! Say you will help me!* And out of the corner of his eye he could see his aunt's smug triumph as she faced her stepdaughter. Groaning inwardly, he forced himself to smile at Hannah.

"Did not Harriet tell you?" he heard himself saying. "I find myself quite in need of a cat, actually—mice, you know."

It was as though a great sigh of relief escaped Harriet, and the color flooded back into her face. Her dark eyes brimmed with gratitude, and he felt somehow rewarded for his effort. But Hannah fixed him with a disbelieving stare.

"You have driven all the way to Rowe's Hill for a *cat*?" she demanded awfully. "I cannot credit it— 'tis a Banbury tale if ever I heard one, Richard Standen! Farms are full of the creatures—indeed, they are everywhere! And you cannot say . . ." She goggled, overcome by a rare loss of words.

Richard's gaze dropped to the tiny claw marks on the back of his hand. "But I fancied a black one."

"Three." Harriet smiled crookedly at him from her seat down the table. "I believe you said you would take three."

"Did I? I say, but I don't . . ." The mute appeal in her eyes was again unmistakable, prompting him to sigh. "Oh, yes—three," he capitulated gracefully.

" 'Tis settled, then," Sir John announced, firmly dismissing the unpleasant subject. "Well, now, let's have no more talk of cats in this house. I for one am for my dessert and a bit of port afterward. What say you, Thornton—care to stay for a glass?"

Later, as he passed Harriet on his way to her father's library, Richard's mouth twisted wryly as he hissed for her ears alone, "You wretch—you scheming little minx! What the devil am I to do with three cats?"

"Keep them alive," she whispered back.

"You are beholden to me for this, Harry—I know not how or when, but I mean to be repaid. Cats!"

Hannah's head went back at the sound of Harriet's answering giggle, and as soon as the men were out of earshot she retorted tartly, "Well, I suppose it makes more sense for him to want a mouser than to come to see you, after all. A man like Richard Standen is above your touch, missy, and don't you forget it."

"Of course, Mama. I am not such a fool as to cast out lures to him, if that is what you are insinuating."

"Humph! See as you don't, then. You've a far better chance with Mr. Thornton, I can tell you." Rising stiffly, the older woman leaned on a chair, her back to Harriet. "You will retire for the night, of course."

"You do not wish me to entertain Mr. Thornton?" Harriet asked with feigned innocence. "But I thought—"

"I do not wish you putting yourself before my nephew like a shameless baggage," Hannah responded coldly. "Good night."

Thwarted in his efforts to share Two Harry with Harriet, Richard rose early and considered the possibility of escaping without the three cats. But he knew now that to do so would seal the fate of the poor animals, and while he held no affection for them, he was not cruel. Besides, he did owe Harriet a favor, after all. Without her generosity, Two Harry would not exist for him, and that horse meant next to everything to him. Two Harry was going to make him the envy of every sporting blood in England, he was certain.

With that in mind, he came downstairs ready to leave, telling himself that three cats were a small sacrifice for a bang-up racehorse. Already in the front hall, Harriet and Thomas were disputing the means of transporting the animals, with the footman's stoutly maintaining that the basket on his arm was quite the only one Lady Rowe would allow.

"But it has no lid!" Richard heard his step-cousin protest. "You cannot take kittens in a basket with no lid in a carriage, else they—"

"Er, I rather thought to put them in the boot," Richard interrupted.

"The boot? Nonsense! 'Tis cold and they would freeze." She dismissed the notion with a forcefulness he'd not seen in her in years.

He approached the basket warily, wondering again at what he'd done, only to be reassured somewhat by the sight of a rather large gray tabby curled against the small black kitten and a tiny mottled calico one that could only be described as an acutely ugly runt. Without thinking, Richard poked the little calico with a fingertip.

"Harry, this has to be the ugliest creature I have ever been privileged to see," he complained. "He won't even have to actually catch the mice to kill them."

"She. Calicos are females, Richard. And positively homely kittens sometimes grow into beautiful animals."

He eyed the small furball skeptically for a moment, and as if it knew it were the subject of discussion, the kitten opened its eyes to look back at him. One eye was blue and the other was yellow.

"Harry, its eyes do not even match."

She lifted the tiny orange-and-black-and-white kitten from the basket and rubbed its nose against hers. "Heloise is quite the sweetest-tempered creature you will ever encounter, Richard. She cannot help it if she looks as though she were naught but patches of colors."

"Heloise?"

"Yes." She laid the kitten back in the basket and pointed to the other two. "The mama is Athena, because she is positively wise—she knows when you are blue-deviled or out of reason cross and she always soothes, and the black one is Abelard."

"So named for his piety?" he cut in with a hint of sarcasm.

"Well, I never thought of Abelard as particularly pious," she murmured. "There was Heloise, after all."

"Yes, well, I am willing to wager *that* Heloise had more to recommend her than this one." He looked up at the footman, who still held the blanket. "Put them in the carriage, then, my good fellow, but see that they are on the floor." To Harriet he added, "I did not come all this way to discuss cats, Harry. I've something of a more important nature to tell you."

"Oh . . . oh, yes. Well, we can speak in the front saloon, I believe, for Hannah is not yet down."

Her manner had changed once again, becoming more tentative. Impulsively he reached for her arm. "You must not let her overset you so, Harry. Stand up to her—'tis the only way. Otherwise you will be under thumb forever."

She looked down at his fingers on her elbow. "Do you think I have not tried? Do you think I did not fight her at first? 'Twas so long ago, but I still remember the birchings she gave me to improve my character, Richard, and I still remember that my father will always agree with her to keep his peace." Her voice had dropped to little more than a whisper. "I . . . I know you must think me a silly, weak creature, but I can do naught but hate her in silence, God forgive me."

"Harry . . . Harry . . ."

"Why do you think it was that George left?" she demanded passionately. "He took the only opportunity that presented itself to leave this place. Oh, how I would that I were a man and I could escape also. But the only escape for me is to take Edwin Thornton, and . . . and I cannot do it."

"Could you not go to George?"

"I have not his direction, I fear, for he is not the least good at writing letters. Besides, I doubt he would be wishful of having a sister hanging on his sleeve. No, when he was safely gone from here, he forgot what he left behind—and well he should. She was not kind to him either."

"I'm sorry, Harry."

The kindness in his voice was almost more than she could bear. "No." She shook her head determinedly, as though she would not accept his pity. " 'Tis not your concern, Richard. If I am to come about, I will have to think of something on my own." She pulled away from him and walked resolutely toward the front saloon. "Now, I'd hear of Two Harry, if you do not mind telling me of him."

"You are certain? There was so much to say that I could not convey in the letter, but perhaps you would not wish to hear of anything so trivial."

"Oh, no! I assure you that 'tis not the case in the least! Owning half a racehorse, even one that has not yet raced, is far more exciting than anything I have ever done, Richard. No, you must not think I am not interested! Indeed, I just wish 'twere possible to see him myself."

"He's a beauty, Harry—sleek and bred to run. Even with the bad weather last week, I watched him run along the hedgerows at Richlands, and he is as fast as the wind. I—we—shall be the envy of every racing buck in the country, I can tell you."

"I shall pray he wins."

"You'll not need to pray, Harry—he's a natural racer. I have already engaged the best trainer I could find, and I think I have located an experienced jockey to ride him. Indeed, the most important thing left is to determine our colors, and I wanted you to choose them." His blue eyes betrayed the excitement he felt whenever he spoke of the horse. "He is, after all, half yours."

"You wish me to choose the racing colors? Richard, I . . . well, I have not the least notion, and—"

"Surely you have two favorite hues that, done in satin, would look distinctive."

"Actually, I like rose and green—deep green—but 'tis scarce what I would think of for—"

"Rose and green it is, then." His eyes fairly danced as they met hers. "Two Harry will race under rose and green."

"Will it be expensive—the colors, the jockey, the trainer? There is still the other thousand, Richard."

"No. 'Tis well-known that I stand to inherit the Standen fortune in a matter of weeks now, so 'tis simple enough to ask them to wait for their money. Indeed, I had thought to offer to repay you."

"Oh, no—no, I pray you will not," she responded quickly. "Richard, I quite meant what I said: the notion that I actually own a portion of a real racehorse affords me an enjoyment that my money could not. Besides . . ." An impish smile played at the corners of her mouth. "Besides, you have saved my cats."

"You know, Harry, sometimes I think that beneath that cowed and meek exterior there lurks a bit of a baggage in you," he teased.

"If so, you must surely be the only one to see it, I fear, for Edwin Thornton seems to think me as dull as he is."

"Harry . . ." His manner changed, growing serious. "Harry, no matter what they do to you, do not let Aunt Hannah or Uncle John force you into a marriage with Thornton. The man's naught but a pompous ass."

"I have already made myself plain on that head, Richard, and with your taking the cats, there's naught else she can threaten to do to me. But I shall miss them terribly—I shall. I had come to rely on Athena to lift my spirits, you know," she added wistfully.

"Perhaps she would let you keep the one, then. I could speak with her, and—"

"No. Just promise me that you will take care of them—'tis all I ask."

"Well, they will not go hungry," he assured her.

"And you will not stick them out in a barn or stable somewhere, will you?"

"Dash it, Harry—they're cats!" Then he noted the reproach in those dark eyes of hers, and he relented, sighing. "All right—so long as they do not stay underfoot, they can come in the house."

"Word of a gentleman?"

"Word of a gentleman. Does that satisfy you?"

It was her turn to sigh. "It has to, I suppose. But, no, it does not. If I had any say in the matter, I should keep them, of course."

"Harriet!"

Hannah Rowe's imperious voice reverberated down the hallway, penetrating even the walls of the front saloon. Harriet blanched visibly. "Oh, dear. I have to go, else she will be angered I am here. Godspeed you safely, Richard."

"Angered?"

"She does not think it meet that I should speak with a man unattended in a closed room."

"Harry, I am your cousin, and—"

"My step-cousin." Her eyes darted warily toward the door. "Please—I have to go."

"I mean to speak to Uncle John of this," he muttered grimly. " 'Tis not right."

"I pray you will not—you can only make my situation worse. Good-bye, Richard."

Outside in the hall, he overheard Hannah demanding to know where she'd been, but he couldn't determine Harriet's low response. And the injustice of it all made him seethe. But she was right: there was little enough he could do to change things for her.

He waited until their footsteps receded to the back of the house before leaving the small parlor, and then he followed them to take his formal leave. That done, he escaped the house she could not, and gratefully swung up into one of his carriage seats. On the floor, the three cats yawned and stretched against the woolen blanket that lined the basket, as though they did not know they had acquired an extremely reluctant owner.

It was not until he'd traveled several miles, his thoughts still troubled by Harriet's pitiful existence, that he realized that the small calico kitten had managed to climb onto the seat beside him. Emboldened, she edged even closer, until, before he knew it, she'd managed to snuggle against his leg.

"Get off," he ordered sternly.

For answer, she climbed upon his thigh as though she owned it. And while he watched balefully, she adjusted her small body until it suited her, stretching to span the width of his leg, purring all the while.

"Get off, I said!" He started to knock her from her perch, only to remember how anxious Harry had been to secure the cats' home with him. Gingerly he tried to lift the kitten without pulling the threads in his expensive trousers but obviously Heloise had other ideas. Her small claws took hold, grasping his skin through the cloth, opening and closing, whilst she still purred.

"Can we not call a truce?" he offered hopefully. "You get off me and back into the basket, and I will forget that you have covered me with hair."

She released her claws, but rather than relinquishing her place, simply rolled over belly-up and stretched coquettishly, much as he'd seen more than one woman do in bed.

"Heloise, huh? You have about as much claim to beauty as a London urchin, you know." But his hand inadvertently crept to touch the softness of her long, fluffy fur. "Just do not be forgetting that I dislike cats intensely. And do not be thinking you are going anywhere but the cellars at Richlands."

To which Heloise responded by bathing his hand with an incredibly rough tongue.

4 It was almost two months before Richard wrote again, this time to tell Harriet that Two Harry's progress was such that he was planning to begin the circuit at Newmarket, testing the colt in the overnight races before trying for the bigger purses. In the meantime, he was taking the opportunity of running against any and all of his Sussex neighbors foolish enough to bet against Two Harry. So far, he'd collected well over her thousand pounds in winnings, and would send her half wherever she wished, but he suspected her bank in London would be best. Would she advise if that were satisfactory? Oh, and if everything went as planned, he meant to bring the horse to Rowe's Hill when he came to seek final settlement of his father's estate from Sir John. It was, after all, not all that far from Newmarket itself, and he meant to come just before Opening Day. They could discuss further how she wished the accounting of future winnings then.

She had to suppress a smile, for it was obvious that he never truly considered that Two Harry could lose, while she was enough of a pragmatist to expect he would—at least some of the time. After all, their horse was still, for the most part, an untried two-year-old. In the chill March dampness of her chamber, she drew her coverlet about her, settled back against the pillows of her bed, and continued reading.

As for your cats, my dear Harriet, I can only tell you that they have put my household at sixes and sevens. My housekeeper abhors them, my cook prepares full-course dinners for them, and my valet despairs at the hairs they leave everywhere. But try as we might, we have failed to convince the creatures that they are not privileged with the run of the house. And your Heloise, shameless hussy that she is, seems to think the best bed to be had is atop my feet. She waits until all are asleep before she creeps onto my coverlet, and there seems to be no stopping the furry chit. Locked doors positively inspire her to hide Godknows-where, that she may find me at night. And Abelard has taken to attacking the downstairs maids, lying in wait behind the curtains, and then preening himself when they screech. Truth to tell, only your Athena seems to have been born with any manners. You know not how many times I have wished you were here, that I might cheerfully throttle you, you wretch.

But it was obvious that the coming racing season was never far from his thoughts even in a letter. He'd finished by enclosing two pieces of rose and dark green satin, saying he hoped she approved their colors, and then had signed himself "Your affectionate cousin, Richard Standen." A boldly scrawled postscript added, "And I take leave to tell you that not one of the creatures you have foisted on me is the least mouser." The telltale smudge of a partial pawprint graced the outside of the envelope.

She laid the letter aside, sighing. While she was

gratified that her cat and kittens were safely ensconced at Richlands, she nonetheless missed them terribly. And she wished—oh, how she wished—that she could see Two Harry. To her, Richard's life seemed to be the epitome of all that was fashionable and exciting, whilst her own was exceedingly dull and empty.

A sharp rap at her chamber door brought her up from her self-pity, and she barely had time to retrieve Richard's letter and slip it under her pillows before Hannah entered the room. For once, her stepmama was wearing a rare smile, but Harriet nonetheless was wary.

"So you have heard from that scapegrace nephew of mine again, have you?"

"Richard? Yes." Then, fearing to be questioned at length as to the nature of the letter, Harriet hastened to add, "He did but write to tell me of the cats, after all. 'Twould seem he has some affection for them."

"Nonsense. 'Tis a Banbury tale if he wrote it, for 'tis only you who are silly over the dirty little beasts. Ten to one, he has them in the barn and stables where they belong." Hannah, about to launch once again into a tirade against what she considered her stepdaughter's weakness, caught herself and managed to smile yet again. "Well, 'tis of no matter anyway, for they are gone from here. And I have news of far greater import, I am sure." She paused, waiting for Harriet to respond. And when the younger woman did not, she announced in triumph, " 'Tis all but settled between Mr. Thornton and your papa, my dear—a summer wedding, I believe—and I am taking you all the way to Norwich for the ordering of your brideclothes. I would not have it said we behaved shabbily to you on your marriage, after all, and—"

"I have no wish to wed Edwin Thornton," Harriet cut in tiredly. "Indeed, I shall not."

The curve of Hannah's forced smile flattened as she drew her mouth into a thin, disapproving line. "Nonsense," she dismissed simply.

"I will not."

"It is your dear papa's express wish to see you settled, after all, and—"

"And Edwin and I should not suit."

"Nonetheless, you will accept his generous offer, Harriet," Hannah stated coldly, all pleasantness now gone from her face. "He settles five hundred pounds on you, which is commendable, given that you are twenty-four years of age and past the bloom of your youth. And he is possessed of a large, commodious house, of which you shall be mistress."

"But I dislike Edwin Thornton! He is naught that I would have for a husband—can you and Papa not see that?"

"We can see an undutiful daughter, miss!" Hannah retorted. "You will accept your papa's choice for you, and that is that!"

A summer wedding. A summer wedding to a man she detested and could not love. Richard Standen's words echoed in Harriet's ears. *Harry, no matter what they do to you, do not let Aunt Hannah or Uncle John force you into a marriage with Thornton.* But despite her brave words to the contrary, she was by no means certain that she had the strength to defy them. Indeed, she had no illusions that her refusal would not be greeted by reprisals from the both of them. And Hannah Rowe could be calculatingly vicious when crossed.

Never. Never. She wanted to cry out that she'd never care for the likes of a man like Edwin Thornton, but the words would not come. Her mind groped for the means to refuse his suit without completely angering Hannah.

"Well, miss—is aught wrong with your tongue? Or have you been attending what I've said at all?" her stepmama demanded, her patience now at an end. "Answer me!"

" 'Tis so sudden. I—"

"Sudden! Four years! Four years, missy—and you would deem it sudden? For four years Edwin Thornton has tried to fix his interest with you, and you've done naught but dissemble where he is concerned! Well, there's an end to it, and 'tis now!"

Harriet's worst fear had come to pass, cornering her. She felt suddenly sick, but her mind still sought the means of avoiding the marriage. Time. Time— that was it; she needed time to escape. And if she appeared to set her will against Hannah's, there'd be no time. Indeed, she had not a doubt that if her stepmama had her way, she'd be wed by special license that very day. Her dark eyes brimming with welling tears, her chin quavering despite the fact that she bit her lip to maintain her composure, she somehow managed to nod.

" 'Tis better, miss!" Hannah snapped. And then with the triumph came a slight softening, prompting her to reach a hand to Harriet's shoulder. "Come, there will be a day when you will thank me for this—a day when you are mistress of your own home." She gave the younger woman a brief, awkward pat before turning to leave. "You must make a list of what you will need."

"When . . . when is the wedding?" Harriet choked out.

"As to that, I should expect the banns to be cried and a decent interval to pass so as to assure everyone that all is as it ought to be. A hasty marriage for one your age would be certain to cause undue comment." Turning briefly back to her step-daughter, Hannah added, "I should think it July or August even, but that is between your papa and Mr. Thornton." And as she looked back at the bed, she caught sight of the two splashes of color spilling from beneath the coverlet. "What is that?" she demanded.

Harriet's fingers closed over the swatches of satin, drawing them out. "Oh . . . d-did I not tell you? Sherborne has bought his racehorse, and he s-sends me samples of his colors. They are quite p-pretty, do you not think?"

"Humph! A racehorse! 'Tis as your papa says, I fear: within a twelvemonth, Sherborne will have run through the Standen fortune"—Hannah sniffed—"squandered in gaming and on his bits of fluff, I am sure. According to Mrs. March, when she was in London last, his pursuit of an opera dancer was the *on-dit*—not to mention the crim. con. about Lady Buckhampton!" She caught herself, sniffing again. "But I am sure that whatever he does cannot reflect on the Belfords, after all, but will be remarked to the Standen side of his nature."

"Cousin Richard would not—"

"Shows what you would know of such things, missy! Even if he is my nephew, he is a Standen also—and they are as like as peas in a pod! And with his looks and now his fortune, you can be sure that all manner of opera dancers are casting out lures to him!"

With that emphatic pronouncement, Hannah left, closing the door behind her, leaving Harriet to sort out her unhappy thoughts. And while she did not entirely doubt what her stepmama had said about Richard, she found it difficult to reconcile her image of him with that of a heartless rake. But she had more pressing problems just now, she re-

minded herself severely. She could not, she would
not wed Edwin Thornton—she'd rather be dis-
graced than married to such a pompous clod-pole.

Slowly a desperate plan evolved in her mind.
She'd write to Plimly immediately, begging to come
to her and her sister at Bath. She'd have to think
of an excuse—an invitation to the wedding, perhaps
—else she could not be certain that Hannah would
allow a letter to be sent. The lowering thought that
life with two quite elderly, dithery old women might
prove tedious crossed her mind and was quickly
replaced by the realization that nothing could be
worse than her lot at Rowe's Hill.

Her greatest fear outside of discovery was that
perhaps something might have changed, that
perhaps Plimly might no longer want her to come.
And if that should be the case, she was in the basket
indeed. In her mind's eye she could see what life
with Edwin would be. She'd never want for anything, 'twas true, but then, she'd never be allowed
another thought of her own either. And while her
knowledge of the intimacies required of the married
state was sketchy at best, somehow she could not
imagine allowing him to touch her person. A
shudder of distaste traveled the length of her spine,
sending a wave of nausea through her. No, Edwin
Thornton was not what she wanted in a husband.

For a brief moment she looked down at the scraps
of satin still in her hand and dared to dream. No,
if she were to wed at all, she should like to have a
man like Richard Standen. The image of the
handsome viscount floated to mind, blotting out
that of the stolid Mr. Thornton. Now, there was the
man of girlish dreams, if ever there was one. His
bright blue eyes sparkled with mischief and
laughter, his dark hair curled boyishly, framing
quite the best face of her memory, while his broad

shoulders gave him a masculinity that Edwin somehow lacked despite a certain thickness there. But it was Richard himself rather than his looks that truly drew her to him. He might be all that Hannah said of him, but to her he'd always been kindness itself. From childhood, he'd teased gently, listened willingly, and acted as her friend. But Hannah's words, recalled now, somehow stabbed at her heart.

With his looks and now his fortune, you can be sure that all manner of opera dancers are casting out lures to him! And as the pain grew with the realization that it was probably true, Harriet admitted to herself for the first time why it hurt so much. She loved Richard Standen—and had since she'd been the little girl in the torn dress. She'd loved him from the moment he turned back that day, risking his own life and limbs to save her from her papa's bull. She drew her legs up under the coverlet and hugged them, savoring the newness of discovered love. For a time she allowed herself the luxury of remembering the scrapes, the kindnesses offered a skinny little girl, the smiles, the shared amusements of fourteen years past.

But the discovery was soon followed by despair, and her spirits plummeted. If there were any certainty in this life, it was that Richard Standen did not share her regard—oh, he liked her well enough as a step-cousin, but as for his kindnesses to her, they were more in the nature of friendship, or perhaps even pity for her circumstances. And his ready smile was probably bestowed on everyone—indeed, it was much of his charm that he was not high in the instep in the least. No, while he liked her well enough, he cherished not the least passion for her. And she was certainly neither accomplished enough nor pretty enough to ever expect anything else.

But she could not marry Edwin Thornton. Reluctantly she turned her thoughts once again to the problem at hand. Throwing back the covers, she rose to fetch the small writing desk she'd received from the Misses March one Christmas, and sitting on the side of her bed, she composed a letter to Miss Plimly and her sister. They were, she sighed to herself, her best hope. She'd take her remaining thousand pounds and flee to them if all else failed. Actually, her fifteen hundred pounds, for she had Two Harry's first winnings also.

As she finished writing, she could hear voices from downstairs. Her fingers blue from the cold, she chafed them over the candle used to heat the wax for the seal and listened as her papa bombastically informed the newly arrived Mr. Thornton that his daughter would be pleased to accept his offer. Let them think what they would, she muttered to herself. Let them discover that a reluctant betrothal was not a marriage. She ought to feel guilty for misleading Edwin Thornton, she supposed, but as she thought of his overweening conceit again, she felt justified in what she'd done. She'd bought herself several months of peace in which to plot her escape, and escape she would.

All too soon she heard her father call upstairs, bawling out to her, "Harriet! Harriet! Come down this instant, I tell you! You have a caller of import!"

With a sigh, she slid off the bed, and without bothering to smooth the wrinkles from her faded blue gown, she muttered under her breath, "I am coming, Papa." Squaring her shoulders resolutely, she opened her door and stepped out into the hallway, hoping fervently that Edwin Thornton would not expect to kiss her.

5 March passed with no word from either Miss Plimly or her sister, and as April brought forth its interminable showers, Harriet worried that somehow her letter had been lost. She followed it with two more and waited, avoiding her unwanted betrothed whenever she dared. As for Edwin Thornton, he confined his displays of affection to an occasional pat on the arm and one brief kiss on the cheek. Edwin, as usual, appeared determined to be an utter pattern-card of propriety, and for that, at least, Harriet was grateful.

The news of their betrothal was accepted quietly throughout the neighborhood, for there did not seem to be much remarkable about the match, except for the fact that the bride had been thought to be securely on the shelf. Several social events, all small and subdued, were hosted by the vicar, Harriet's father and stepmother, and various of the local gentry in honor of the occasion, but other than that, little changed for Harriet. Not quite true, she forced herself to admit as she allowed Edwin to assist her into his rather soberly appointed carriage one evening on their way to a pre-Season party at Squire March's comfortable home. No, Hannah was almost pleasant for the first time since she'd discovered herself saddled with an unwanted stepdaughter fourteen years earlier. And as she adjusted the slim skirt of the new blue-figured muslin about her legs, Harriet had to admit her usually clutch-fisted stepmother had actually spent money to clothe her more suitably, if not actually fashionably.

Edwin, unfortunately, after having kept polite distance from his betrothed for a full month and more, took this particular evening to assert himself beyond mere opinion. Reaching across the seat to squeeze her hand, he allowed his fingers to linger on hers.

"You look uncommonly handsome tonight, my dear," he murmured, moving forward until his knee touched hers. And, emboldened by her lack of response, he leaned even closer, until she was nearly overwhelmed by the heavy cologne he wore. She closed her eyes to quell the nausea that rose as the thick, overpowering, sweet smell engulfed her, and was startled by the feel of his rather flaccid, moist lips on hers. And within the instant he was across the seat, his arms sliding awkwardly about her shoulders, pulling her closer as he planted several wet kisses on her mouth and cheek.

Caught entirely off her guard, she stiffened briefly, fighting the revulsion she felt, and then she began to struggle, turning her head and trying to disentangle herself from his arms. His breath, still smelling of her father's brandy, rushed against her face.

"Mr. Thornton . . . sir, please!" She wriggled free by delivering a sharp blow with her elbow into his arm and then ducking away. "Really, sir, but—"

"Dash it, Miss Rowe, but we are betrothed! 'Tis to be expected—"

"I do not believe I gave you leave to take liberties with my person, sir," she reminded him acidly.

For a moment his eyes glittered in the faint evening light, almost frightening her, but then he recovered himself and slid back into his own seat. Readjusting his plain neckcloth, he managed to apologize, "Your pardon, my dear, but I have waited four years for the day when I can call you mine own." Taking out his handkerchief, he wiped his mouth. "A few more months cannot be so long, I suppose," he added grudgingly.

A few months. Panic assailed her at the thought. "Mr. Thornton, I—"

"I did not mean to overset you, my dear—I pray you will forgive the lapse. A gently bred female such as yourself cannot know how 'tis for a man." He possessed one of her hands again, this time with his usual limp grasp. "Indeed, your maidenly reserve pleases me, Harriet, and I look forward to the time when I may instruct you as my wife. It must be the new dress," he finished lamely, dropping her hand when she did not respond as he had hoped.

"Mr. Thornton—"

"You are not like the other females of my acquaintance—creatures more interested in fancy dresses, balls, and routs," he continued, ignoring her attempts at interruption. "You are a sensible woman, devoid of silly romantical notions, and for that I should honor you."

She wanted to scream out that she *wanted* fancy dresses, wanted to attend more than quiet neighborhood parties, wanted the fashionable life she'd only read of, and that she did indeed cherish romantical notions also, but she knew he was incapable of understanding anything beyond what he wished. Aloud she murmured, "Alas, but you cannot know me well if you think—"

"Nonsense. I have observed you these four years

past and have discovered in you that which pleases me most—you are quiet and sensible and not overly given to levity."

"And that is what you desire in a wife?" she asked incredulously.

"And you do not put yourself forward—you have been well-schooled to respect those above you." He leaned back, his sober face made even more so by the shadows that played across it. "There is, however, the matter of your two thousand pounds, of course. I've been meaning to broach that subject for some time." When she did not respond, he quickly pursued the matter. "I cannot credit that your father has allowed you a free hand with so much money, my dear, and I cannot think it wise of him, when—"

"My father had little choice—the money is and shall remain mine, Mr. Thornton," she interrupted with dampening finality.

"But it must needs to be invested, my dear—you should have the wise counsel of a man, that it may grow and perhaps provide a settlement for your children one day."

"It *is* invested."

Too obtuse to note the decided edge to her voice, Edwin Thornton dismissed the notion that she could possibly know what she was about. "Even so, I should like . . . that is to say, I should *expect* even to manage the sum for you, my dear, and—"

"Edwin, you sound much like a gazetted fortune-hunter—which I should not like to think you," she retorted. "The money I have is my mother's portion to me, and as she saw fit to leave it under chancery law for my 'sole and separate use,' there's naught you or my father has to say in the matter, is there?" she added firmly.

"Well, I am sure . . ." He drew back even further,

stung, his chagrin evident. "Far be it from me to attempt to profit from your mother's portion, Harriet. I did but wish to guide you for the sake of our children."

"We have no children."

"But in the course of time . . ."

By the stiffness of his speech and manner, she knew he was deeply affronted, but she didn't care in the least. He was encroaching in the extreme, and had she been able to think of one, she'd have given him a sharp set-down. Instead, she turned her attention to the carriage window.

"I shall hope that in the course of our marriage, you will come to accept my guidance in all things, Harriet," he said finally, sighing heavily.

She closed her eyes and prayed that Plimly would answer soon. Surely three letters could not have all gone astray.

Conversation at the Marches was dull, insipid, and boring for the most part, with the females of the neighborhood collecting in one room whilst their male counterparts disputed Liverpool's tax plan for the country's recovery from the Napoleonic wars in another. And as expected, Miss Emma March spent the better part of the evening regaling the younger girls with her accounts of the previous London Season. Since only Harriet, Mrs. March, and Mrs. Wickstead were old enough to be out of the schoolroom, the others hung avidly on every word, gazing with a mixture of admiration and envy at one who'd actually completed a Season. That Emma had not taken did not matter—she'd been *there.* Besides, she was to accompany her younger sister, Faith, again this year, and Mrs. March had hinted rather broadly that there was a particular gentleman . . .

Harriet was heartily sick of the self-centered silliness of Emma's conversation, and her mind wandered inattentively until she realized that the younger girl now spoke of Richard. And her heart sank as she discovered that the insipidly lovely Miss March thought to bring her step-cousin up to scratch this time.

"La, but I shall never forget standing up at Almack's with Sherborne, you may be sure," Emma recalled, her pale blue eyes taking on a faraway expression. "He is quite the best dancer, you know, and exceedingly handsome. I recall that he stood up with me a full three times in one evening, and Mama—" She stopped, casting a surreptitious look at Mrs. March, and then went on. "Mama thought he meant to fix his interest with me then. I tried to tell her he was but a prodigious flirt, but she reminded me that gentlemen—even the rakish ones—do not demonstrate such a particularity without reason, after all."

"Still, he did not offer," her sister, Faith, reminded her, gaining a glare from Miss March.

"He was called away to the sickbed of a dear friend, I believe," Emma explained blithely. "A Mr. Hawleigh, it was."

"And you heard Papa: 'Sherborne is naught but an outrageous flirt,' he told you and Mama," Faith persisted.

"He stood up with me three times. That signifies—"

"What fustian! You and Mama should listen to Papa," the younger girl snorted. "He said ten to one it was but—"

"You were not there," Emma retorted haughtily. "You cannot know how it was."

"Well, I should not refine so much on an evening at Almack's, you may be sure," Faith sniffed.

Mrs. March, her attention drawn away from the litany of Mrs. Wickstead's humors of the liver, sought to end the matter quickly. "Faith," she ordered sternly, "you must not overset your sister. It does not become you to dispute what you do not know." Then, tittering as though she harbored some secret, she confided to the rest of the ladies present, "Sherborne *was* most particular in his attention, to be sure, and if poor Mr. Hawleigh—"

Harriet had heard enough. That Richard had known the Marches since Emma was but a skinny, pale child also seemed to lend a certain authenticity to the story. Her stomach churned at the thought that her dashing step-cousin could even consider an empty-headed widgeon—even a beautiful empty-headed widgeon—like Emma March. But stranger matches had been made, and there was no accounting for the tastes of men, when one viewed the matter dispassionately. Still, it looked to her as though Sherborne could have done better—he was, after all, a viscount, and Emma March merely the daughter of a wealthy country gentleman.

"La," Mrs. March continued happily, "I should not be saying it, but Sherborne is to come here this very month."

The ratafia Harriet had been sipping suddenly tasted like vinegar in her mouth, and she fought the urge to be sick. Richard must have written to Emma March also. And somehow the thought that he was not coming just to see Harriet was quite lowering. But it made sense: Richard would come to Rowe's Hill to gain his inheritance, and then he would offer for Emma. And if he showed Two Harry to his step-cousin, well, it was but a courtesy to a business partner.

Pressing her temples and closing her eyes to shut out the thought of Richard's becoming betrothed to Emma, Harriet leaned forward in her chair. Faith was the first to note her distress.

"Are you all right, Miss Rowe? Mama, I think dear Harriet is not feeling quite the thing just now."

Opening her eyes, Harriet found herself the object of curiosity, and color flooded her face. "No . . . no, that is, I have the headache."

" 'Tis the abominable weather," Mrs. March decided. To which Mrs. Wickstead nodded, launching into yet another catalog of her own megrims caused by the inclement weather. But Faith sat down on the small sofa beside Harriet and felt her forehead. "I think perhaps she is becoming ill—perhaps a fever."

"Oh, dear." Mrs. March came to peer at Harriet, her own forehead furrowed with a frown. "Yes, well, 'tis to be hoped 'tis not contagious. Emma, seek out Mr. Thornton and tell him his betrothed is not at all well. Yes, yes—tell him that he must needs escort her home." That settled, she turned back to Mrs. Wickstead. "My dear, you suffer from the headache frequently? I simply must share with you the remedy Knighton prescribed for me when we were in London."

Faith slid closer, murmuring, "Do not be telling Sir John and Lady Rowe about what Emma said, for I think it all hum anyway. From what Papa says, Sherborne is as like to offer for Em as the Prince Regent himself, but Mama refines too much on every smile. And Sherborne *is* said to be a shocking flirt, from all I have heard from Em's friends—'tis why the ladies all have their caps set for him. I'd not have your parents know just how foolish Mama and Em are."

"I do not refine much on gossip," Harriet assured her gratefully.

"If you have something to say, Faith, I would that

you came out and said it," Mrs. March chided. " 'Tis impolite to be forever mumbling."

" 'Twas nothing of import, Mama. I did but wish dear Harriet a quick recovery," Faith answered glibly.

And in the carriage returning to Rowe's Hill, Edwin Thornton was less than pleased to have been removed from the agreeable company of his neighbors, particularly since he'd considered that he'd been waxing especially eloquent on the short-comings of Liverpool's government. Instead of offering his betrothed comfort in her distress, he remarked rather peevishly, "You did not appear ill earlier, my dear."

"It came on me suddenly."

"Yes, well, I hope you do not let yourself be given to megrims. It bespeaks of a weakness of character to allow oneself to be governed by one's humors."

There was such self-sure conviction in Edwin Thornton's tone that Harriet, who had in truth never been ill above a day or two in her life, could not resist injecting a little doubt into his mind. "Alas," she sighed weakly, "but I fear I have not the strength of character you possess, dear Mr. Thornton, for I have been plagued with these distressful headaches all of my life. Indeed, there are times when I am forced to take to my bed for days until they leave."

"Nonsense!" he responded briskly. "The cure for such things is to ignore them."

"No, it does not serve. The only relief I get is to burn feathers and camphor pastilles in my chamber."

Apparently daunted by thoughts of the terrible smell such a combination conjured up, her betrothed lapsed into silence. It was not until they reached the lane to Rowe's Hill that he spoke again, and this time it was to note the elegant black lacquered carriage drawn up beneath the lamps at the front door.

"Deuced queer time for a visit," he murmured curiously, rousing Harriet from her solitary reverie. "Was your father expecting company?"

"Hmmm? Oh . . ." She leaned forward, straining to see in the dark, and then her heart raced as she recognized Richard Standen's crest. "Oh, 'tis Sherborne come to visit us!"

Her voice betrayed her eagerness to see him again, prompting Mr. Thornton to remark dampeningly, "So I see now. Well, I Have never favored the Corinthian set and cannot understand those who do. Dandies," he pronounced severely, "are naught but fools who waste their substance on frivolity and sports."

"Somehow your opinion does not surprise me, sir," she answered with a tartness that made him frown. But she didn't care. Richard Standen was at Rowe's Hill, and her heart raced at the thought that she would see him again. Her spirits, so lately cast down, rose immeasurably. And then she recalled that he was to visit Emma March also.

6 "Richard! Did you bring him—your race-horse, I mean?" Harriet demanded eagerly of her step-cousin, even before Edwin Thornton could assist her out of her evening cloak.

The viscount, who'd been disputing the timing of his arrival with her father, turned to greet her. And her eagerness restored the humor he'd lost but minutes before.

"Harry! Of course I brought him! 'Tis Opening Day Tuesday at Newmarket, and I'd not miss that for the world—not to mention that I mean to register the colt for the overnights." Then his eyes took in the new cloak as Thornton possessively slipped it from her shoulders, traveling to the new gown beneath. His eyebrow rose in surprise at Hannah's unusual generosity, but his voice was light as he teased, "So 'tis true, after all, Coz—I am to wish you happy?"

Before she could answer, Edwin nodded, speaking for her. "That we are betrothed? Of course 'tis true. You may wish *me* happy, sir!"

The dark brow rose a trifle higher as the blue eyes took in Edwin Thornton's face now. "If you are indeed to wed Harry, I should expect you to be happy," Richard murmured. " 'Tis but that the betrothal surprises me."

As his gaze turned back to her, Harriet colored

uncomfortably. "Well, 'tis not . . . that is to say, 'tis not to be soon."

"Nonsense. Summer will come before you know it, my dear," Edwin asserted, giving her arm yet another proprietary squeeze.

She pulled away from his embrace quickly, stepping back a pace, something that Richard noted. "Could I see him tonight, do you think? I mean, we could take a lantern, and—"

"A horse? My dear, I must protest! The night air is scarce healthful, and besides, dash it, you have the headache!" Edwin reminded her.

"Actually, the night air has revived me." Her eyes met Richard's. "Please—I should like to see your horse."

Sir John looked at his daughter as though she'd taken leave of her senses. "You cannot be serious, missy—'tis raining! Thornton's got the right of it—can't have you getting sick with a wedding to plan. No, no! Look at the animal in the morning, I say! Light's better then anyway."

For the briefest moment rebellion flared in those dark eyes and then faded. Richard's sympathy went out to her, but he'd no wish to make her lot any more difficult. "I'd be happy to show him to you in the morning, Harry."

"I believe her given name is Harriet, sir," Edwin reminded him pompously. "As she is soon to be a married lady, I do not think it proper to call her by other than her given name, my lord."

Richard's jaw tightened perceptibly at the other man's tone. "Harry and I have been friends as well as relations for a long time, Mr. Thornton," he replied coldly. "However, the decision is hers—do you mislike being called Harry, Coz?" he asked, turning again to her.

"I should not wish you to call me anything else,"

she answered promptly, the sparkle returning to her dark eyes. "Indeed, I should be disappointed were you to suddenly decide to become formal with me."

"Then Harry you shall always be to me."

"I say—"

"Er . . ." Sir John, not wanting to allow anything to overset his prospective son-in-law, sought to divert the conversation to a safer topic. "So, you have bought your racehorse after all, Richard. I suppose 'tis not to be wondered at, is it? But 'tis no concern of mine now, I suppose."

"None."

"Well, you cannot say you will not receive every penny Henry left you, sirrah, and more, if the truth be admitted, for I've discharged his trust faithfully. What you do with your fortune now rests on your own head."

"Yes."

"Papa—"

"Oh, yes. Not at all the thing to speak of business in the hall, is it? Yes, well, go on to bed with you, missy," he dismissed her. "And would you gentlemen care for a glass of brandy?"

Edwin, recalling that Miss Rowe was indisposed, decided he'd best drive home before the roads got worse from the rain. Richard declined civilly, offering the fatigue of his journey as an excuse. And with none to drink with him, Sir John was left to retire himself.

Edwin's carriage had scarce left the drive and Sir John had but closed the door to his bedchamber before Harriet heard the rain pelt her window with intensifying force. Gathering her wrapper closer, she laid aside the book she'd taken to bed with her and rose to secure the window before it leaked. But as she reached to hook the lower panel, she heard the sound again. To her surprise, pebbles scattered across the pane and fell against the house. Looking down, she could see that the rain had actually tapered off into a steady drizzle. A lantern bobbed faintly near the bushes.

"What the . . . ?" Gingerly opening the window again, she leaned out for a better look just as another handful of pebbles struck the sill before her.

"Psst! Harry! Over here!"

To her utter amazement, her step-cousin was standing in the wet bushes. "Richard!" she hissed back. "Get out of there—someone will hear you and wonder at it!"

"Do you want to see Two Harry or not?"

"Now?"

"Come on down!"

"Harriet, are you still up?" Hannah called through the door.

"No! That is, I was just retiring, Mama," she answered hastily, withdrawing from the window. "I thought I heard a noise, but 'twas branches against the panes."

"Well, I thought I heard it also, but I daresay you are right."

Apparently the explanation satisfied her stepmama, for she could hear Hannah's slippers pad back down the hall to the opposite end of the house. After holding her breath until she heard the door shut, Harriet leaned out the window again.

"You cannot be serious!"

He held the lantern up and she could see his face. He was grinning boyishly despite the rain that trickled from his black hair. "Come on," he mouthed at her. "You were not always so timid."

It was as though the years rolled away and she was but a little girl again. The cool, damp air floated

in, bringing with it the exhilaration, the rush of
pulse that once had come from daring the
forbidden. She hesitated but momentarily.

"I am in my wrapper. 'Twill take time to—"

He shook his head and motioned to her again.
"You are better covered in that than half the
females I've seen at balls, I swear. Come on!"

With that, she backed away from the window and,
clasping the soft woolen garment closer over her
nightrail, carefully eased the door open. The
hallway was dark and deserted, so dark it gave her
second thoughts. She must have stood there several
minutes trying to screw up her courage, and then
she heard the soft tread of someone creeping up the
stairs. She shrank back, drawing in her breath
sharply.

"Shhhh—'tis only me," Richard whispered. "I
was afraid you'd fallen."

"I couldn't see."

"I left the lantern at the bottom—you have but
to get to the landing to see it." To demonstrate, he
grasped her hand and edged down the darkened
steps before her. At the foot, he stopped to retrieve
his shoes, slipping them on over his wet stockings.

"You'll be carried off with an inflammation of the
lungs," she warned him in a low undervoice.

He shook his head. "As I recall, we were the
healthiest of both our families, Harry." His shoes
on, he again took her hand, pulling her toward the
back of the darkened house, while he held the
flickering lantern to light the way.

There was something quite exciting, something
she'd almost forgotten, about conspiracy. And the
feel of his strong warm fingers over hers sent a
thrill through her. It was as though she did not even
fear to be discovered so long as he was with her.
But that was how it had always been; she'd seldom

hesitated to get into scrapes back when they were children.

The ground was spongy and wet, and the greening grass soaked the hem of her wrapper and nightrail, but she didn't care. She held on and tried to match his longer stride as they walked to her papa's stable. And she was acutely conscious of his masculinity, for he was so unlike Edwin Thornton in every way. For the briefest moment she allowed her fingers to tighten in his.

He stopped to release the bar to the stable door, and the hinges creaked as the door swung outward. "Hold the lantern for a moment, will you?" he whispered as he banged the door shut behind them. "I hope 'twas thought 'twas the wind," he added ruefully, taking the lantern back. "He's in the last stall, for I did not wish him to be made skittish by the others. Tomorrow I am taking him to Squire March's, where he can be stabled alone."

The smell of wet hay and oiled tack and damp horsehair assailed her nostrils. And it was a comforting smell that she'd almost forgotten after Hannah had forbidden her to ride anymore, saying that it was an ungenteel pastime for a lady. And no amount of tears had budged her, nor had the argument that 'twas now fashionable in London to be seen riding in Hyde Park in the mornings. What Hannah decided was law, Harriet recalled bitterly.

"There he is!" he breathed triumphantly, holding the lantern up to illuminate quite the shiniest, sleekest chestnut she'd ever seen. The horse side-stepped around within the narrow confines of the stall, affording her an even better view.

"He . . . he's magnificent, Richard—magnificent!" Without thinking, she reached over the half-door to touch the white spot on the hard bony ridge between the deep brown eyes. The horse's head went back, and then came down again, this time right next to her arm, and she could see 'twas a snowy blaze extended all the way to his nostrils. Her gaze moved eagerly over his sleek, muscular body to the white stockings of his forelegs. He was in truth a magnificent animal.

"He . . . he's perfect, Richard. He's very large for a two-year-old, isn't he?"

"Almost sixteen hands, and as strong as he looks. Wait until you see him run, Harry—he's the fastest I've ever seen, I swear to you. He—"

At that moment she looked up at him, her own dark eyes shining, mirroring his enthusiasm completely. "Oh, I should like it—I should like it above all things!"

The light from the lantern shone on her hair where it streamed, rippling like unbraided silk around her face and over the shoulders of her wrapper. It was a soft, shimmering halo made more gold than brown by the flickering flame. And her upturned face glowed, livened by the light that played across it and by the orange-gold reflection in her eyes. And then the moment was over. She looked away suddenly, the eagerness gone from her voice as she sighed. "But I know 'tis impossible to even think such a thing."

She had been positively pretty then, but as the animation left her, the prettiness faded. And he felt for her keenly, sensing the emptiness of her life.

"Nothing is impossible, Harry," he told her softly.

"You cannot know how—"

"I'd not listen to this." He reached a fingertip to still her lips even as Plimly had done when she was a child. "You can." His eyes gleamed and he nodded as hers widened. "Yes, you can, Harry. You know, just now you were as I remember you—you were the little girl who was wont to follow me without regard to Aunt Hannah or anyone. Do you remember that girl, Harry?"

Tears welled, threatening her composure, and her lower lip trembled as she bit back the urge to cry. His arm slid around her, drawing her closer.

"Harry, don't let anyone rob you of that little girl—not Hannah, not anyone. Not even Thornton."

She wanted to melt against the soft superfine of his coat, to bury her head against his shoulder, but she dared not. She still had his friendship, but if she ever truly unburdened herself, she risked losing even that. Resolutely she stepped back, sniffing.

"You must think me the veriest watering pot, but—"

"I think you half-owner to Two Harry, my dear, and as such, you should see him run."

"Hannah would not allow it, and Papa—"

"They'll never know of it." He lifted up her chin with his knuckle. "Uncle John is not a sporting man, is he? Have you ever known him to go to the races? For a full fifty years and more he's lived not ten miles from Newmarket, and has he attended even once?"

"Never," she admitted.

"If you can concoct a reason to be gone from the house, I intend to see that you are there, Harry. We'll swathe you in veils like a mourning Saracen if we have to, but you are going to see Two Harry run."

"No one is like to recognize me—I have not gone about much." In spite of the impossibility of what he was suggesting, she found herself smiling tremulously. "Indeed, I can think of none of Papa's friends who would even be there—unless 'tis Squire March."

"We'll keep you within my carriage. Even if your

presence occasions comment, none will know your identity," he promised. " 'Twill be said you are my mysterious lady."

"Oh, do you think I could?" Hope rose and then was dashed. "But I have not the least excuse. Hannah does not allow me to go anywhere unattended, and as she does not go anywhere, we both stay at home."

"Visit someone—tell her you are paying a call on someone she mislikes. That should not be so difficult, should it? I cannot imagine that she likes everyone."

"No . . . no, of course not. Indeed, for all that she has positively thrown me at Edwin's head, she cannot abide Mrs. Thornton—says she is an encroaching fool even." And as she said it, she brightened. "Indeed, it could not be thought the least strange that I should wish to visit my future mama-in-law, could it?"

"Not in the least."

"And Hannah would not wish to go, I am certain of it."

"I have never known Aunt Hannah to do anything she does not wish to," he agreed readily. "Then 'tis settled—you are going to Newmarket, Harry."

"But what if she makes me take my maid? Mary would tell, and we should both be in the basket."

"If you would go, you have but to leave that to me. There is something to be said for being Sherborne, after all—Hannah Rowe takes pride in the connection."

"If you would do this for me, I should be grateful to you until my last breath. Oh, Richard! I will not believe it until I am there!"

Two Harry, seemingly bemused by the excitement in her voice, stretched his neck, nudging her. And for answer, she leaned closer, nuzzling his long nose with her cheek. She had a racehorse, and she was going to see him run.

"I think he likes you, Harry," Richard teased.

"And I *love* him!"

"Come on, we'd best get back before you take a chill." He caught her hand again, pulling her away from the horse. "I should hate to have you miss seeing him win the purse."

They walked back to the house quietly, trudging through the mud and wet grass, until they reached the back door. Richard stopped, lifting the lantern to illuminate her face. "Are you really going to marry Thornton, Harry?" he asked suddenly.

"Not if I can avoid doing so."

"Good girl—you should not suit." He dropped her hand. "Go on in—I have to make sure the stable door is locked."

"Wh-why did you ask about Edwin?" She had to know.

"Because I count you as a friend as well as a relation," he answered simply, dashing her hopes.

He'd turned back to the stable, but she was loath to let him go just yet. "Wait—"

He stopped, swinging around to face her again. "What?"

"Tomorrow, will you tell me of the cats—how they fare, I mean?"

"I can tell you now, but I ought to punish you for foisting them off on me." She couldn't quite see his face, but she thought he was grinning. His next words confirmed it. "You wretch—you miserable wretch, Harry. Your Athena is increasing again, or so my cook tells me. And she has no taste whatsoever, for she has bred with the commonest creature from the next house over. As for your Heloise, she is positive that she owns me, whilst

Abelard, who is the only attractive one of the lot, cares only for his food."

"But you like them—admit it."

He cocked his head to one side and appeared to consider. "Like them? I should not go far as that, my dear. Suffice it to say that we have learned to rub along tolerably well together."

"I knew you would like them when you became better-acquainted." Before he could answer, she ran inside, rubbing her cold arms for warmth.

Later, snuggled in the comfort of her feather bed, she pulled her coverlet close and relived every moment. It was foolish to dream of him, she knew, but no one—positively no one—could take her dreams away from her. Not even Emma March.

7 It was with considerable trepidation that Harriet allowed Richard to hand her up into his carriage. Despite the relative ease with which she'd managed to convince Hannah that Mrs. Thornton did indeed wish her presence for the day, she still more than half-expected to be stopped ere they got out of the driveway. But Hannah had not said much, other than to inquire as to why Edwin himself did not come for her.

And it had been so easy to lie that she felt guilty. Edwin, she'd assured her stepmama, had business elsewhere for the day. And indeed he had, for he'd told her he meant to travel to Cambridge to see to new furnishings for the front saloon. It was so typical of Edwin—he'd not bothered to consult her as to her tastes in the matter at all. All that had been needed then to convince Hannah was for Richard to offer to take her as far as the Thorntons', sparing her stepmama the necessity of accompanying her. Indeed, but he would even bring her back when he returned from the races, he promised.

No, all that remained was to pay a short call on Mrs. Thornton so that if the matter ever came up, she could have proof of having been there. For who was likely to ask precisely how long the visit had lasted? With that comforting thought, Harriet settled back against the deep red velvet squabs and tried to forget her qualms.

"Still worried?" Richard asked, smiling at what he considered her groundless fears.

"No," she lied.

The April air was crisp and invigorating, too chilly by half actually, but the heated brick at her feet warmed her feet through her thin kid boots. She slid her hands into the small velvet muff Faith March had given her the past Christmas.

"Cold?"

"A little."

"You will forget the chill when we get there. The excitement will more than keep you warm."

"Where is Two Harry just now?"

"The trainer brings him from Squire March's."

Another reminder that he'd been to see Emma. She sighed and looked out the window, telling herself not to be a fool. One's dreams were on thing, reality quite another. When he'd gone over to the Marches' three days before, she'd longed to ask of Emma, but she'd refrained, telling herself that she didn't really want to know, that she'd hear when the betrothal was announced anyway.

"Why so blue-deviled, Harry? I should have thought you would consider this a splendid adventure," he chided gently.

"I am simply worried about Two Harry, I suppose."

"There's naught to worry you there, I assure you. I was over to see him before daybreak this morning, and he was in fine fettle."

"You went to the Marches' this morning?"

The thought that he could not bear to be away from Emma even one day lowered her spirits even further. But he did not appear to be in the throes of a great passion, or if he were, he certainly made no mention of his love. Finally, after several more minutes of silence, she could bear it no longer.

"And how did you find Emma?" she asked with a casualness she did not feel.

"Who? Oh, I collect you mean the elder Miss March? She is well, I think."

It was hardly a loverlike comment, but one never could tell about gentlemen. Her papa had always said courting was like a card game and that it was better to keep one's hand folded and out of sight—or so he'd told her brother George when George had appeared ready to throw his hat over the windmill for the Rothwell chit.

As though Harriet sought punishment for her thoughts, she persisted. "She is very lovely."

"You think so? I suppose she is," he agreed slowly, reflecting momentartily on Miss Emma March. "But she suffers from a surfeit of conceit."

Surely she had not refused him. Emboldened by his admission that Emma was less than perfection, Harriet leaned across the seat to watch him. "I am told that Incomparables are usually filled with self-consequences," she ventured.

"Most are. However, if you are implying that Miss March is an Incomparable, you are wide of the mark. I can number a dozen girls with better looks and fortunes, Harry. In fact, whatever Miss March has to offer, 'tis more than canceled by her encroaching mama."

"It did not go well for you in that quarter, then," she murmured, settling back.

"Huh? What in the *deuce* are you speaking of?" And then it dawned on him. "You thought I was trying to fix my interest with Miss March?" he demanded awfully. "Harry, what possibly gave you such a foolish notion?"

"Well, did you not stand up with her three times at Almack's? I have heard that bespeaks a particularity that is certain to raise expectations, or have I been told incorrectly?"

"Well, if you had the tale from that harridan who passes for the chit's mama, you have heard only half of the story, believe me. Between the two of them, they set it about that I was ready to pop the question after I took the girl up in my curricle once."

"You didn't stand up with her three times, then?"

"No."

"But Em . . . Miss March said . . ."

"She said what? That I was going to come up to scratch? Harry, I've just come into my inheritance. I've got years before my salad days are over and I am ready for marriage. Despite any number of plots hatched by mother hens, I am not about to part with my fortune for any of their empty-headed daughters just yet. No, you have not to worry that Richard Standen will throw his hat over the windmill and get leg-shackled anytime soon, I can tell you. For one thing, I've got interests . . . that is . . . well, I haven't quite found anyone I'd wish to live with for the rest of my life," he finished quickly. "Just what precisely did Miss March have to say, anyway?"

"Well, I don't know if she said you were offering, exactly, but she certainly gave the impression that you were expected to do so momentarily." Relieved to discover that it was not so, she giggled. "Indeed, the way she said you were coming, 'twas everyone's expectation that you and Em . . . Miss March, that is, were about to make a match of it."

"Egad. Well, her papa cannot think that, for I merely wrote asking him to stable Two Harry whilst I was here. I did not wish the horse to become agitated by that big black of Uncle John's just before the race."

"Oh."

"Ungelded stallions seldom get along at all, you know."

"Yes, Papa says they do not like competition for the mares."

He was peering at her closely now. "You know, if I hadn't known you since you were scarce out of leading strings, I'd think you jealous just now."

"Of course I am jealous!"

"Of Miss March?"

"Yes." And then, fearing she'd revealed too much, she hastened to add, "She had a Season, after all."

"You are jealous because Miss March had a Season? Harry, you would not have liked the Marriage Mart at all. It would have been but a waste of your time and money."

She stared, wounded to the very core of her being. He'd said she would not have taken—that she was not the sort of female to attract anyone but Edwin Thornton. And yet, glutton for punishment that she was, she could not resist asking one final question.

"You do not think I would have found . . . that there would not have been anyone to offer for me, do you?" she asked quietly.

"I think that you would have been miserable. The Marriage Mart is a cruel place where beauty and wealth are placed far above worth. With the clothes that Hannah would have bought you, you would have been pronounced dowdy and forgotten."

"Yes, well . . . I daresay you are right."

It was then that he noted the stricken expression on her face and realized what he had done—and compounded the error rather than rectified it by attempting to explain, "Harry, I did not mean what you think. 'Tis just that the fashionable world would not suit you."

"As if I ever had a chance to discover that!" she cried. "But do not explain as though I am a child! I may not be a beauty, Richard Standen, but I—"

"Harry . . . Harry . . ." He drew one of her hands out of her muff. "You may kick me now, if you think I meant you are plain."

"I know I am plain."

"I have never considered you plain." He cocked his head to one side to study her face, and he realized with a start that he spoke the truth. While brown hair was definitely not the fashion, hers was a soft, shining brown that was rather pleasing. Cropped and curled in the current mode, it would probably be quite attractive. And there was nothing plain about those eyes of hers. Nor about the fine, even features. His eyes dropped lower to her trim, slender figure. "If you were not so shy, and if you had been properly dressed, you would have taken. Indeed, if you were as you were when first I met you, you would have been snapped up by a royal duke probably."

"Do not be funning with me!"

"It was the animation, I think. You used to be so lively, so ready for an adventure. But 'tis not your fault that Hannah destroyed that which she could not accept in you."

"You do not have to make me feel better, Richard."

"Then will you cry friends with me again, Harry? I meant nothing to overset you, you know."

It was impossible to deny the appeal in those blue eyes of his. He could have called her an antidote and she would have still loved him. She forced a smile and nodded. "Friends."

" 'Tis better. For a moment I thought our great

adventure was going to be marred by the blue devils today."

"No. No, of course not."

"I want you to have a splendid time, Harry."

She glanced out the window then and realized they'd passed the village turnoff. "Aren't we going to pay a call on Mrs. Thornton?"

"On the way back. I'd get there early today, as Two Harry runs in the second."

As it was, they arrived to find the stands crowded and the track ringed with vehicles. Luckily Richard's driver managed to squeeze their carriage into line in such a way that Harriet was afforded a clear view of much of the track. As she watched the bustle and excitement of those come to the races, her own excitement mounted. And when Two Harry was led out in the colors she'd chosen, she completely forgot her earlier hurt. Her eyes shone with childlike pleasure as her horse pranced, side-stepping, showing he was eager to run. Clearly he was fresh and in fine fettle. As far as she was concerned, he was quite the prettiest colt there.

Richard leaned across her to point out some of the racing notables and to explain how it was going to be. "He'll race but a mile today, pitted against other two-year-olds registered just yesterday, so the purse will not be as large. But 'twill give me a notion how he runs the track, because I mean to register him for the 2,000 Guineas next year."

"Not this year?"

"He's not eligible until he's three—and besides, the field is determined months in advance. As it is, I was fortunate to get him registered for to-day."

"Oh. I fear I know little of the sport," she admitted self-consciously.

"It doesn't matter—believe me, I have seen enough races for the both of us." Then he saw someone emerge from behind an open curricle. "Wait here—don't leave the carriage," he ordered as he jumped down. "I'll be back as soon as I speak with Cates and Ellis."

"Who?"

"Our trainer and jockey. While you are about it, you might wish to draw that scarf over your face."

Instead, she pressed her nose against the pane until it fogged, watching the men, the horses, and the crowd in the stands. Occasionally she caught glimpses of elegantly dressed females sitting openly, the plumes of their exquisite hats waving in the chill wind. She had never seen the like of any of it.

Her eyes sought Richard where he stood talking to two men dressed in Two Harry's colors, and her heart gave a lurch. He was so tall and well-favored in his dove-gray coat, his snowy shirt, his smooth-fitting trousers, black high-lows, and top hat. If ever there was a Corinthian, it must surely be Richard Standen.

"Sherborne! You running Hawleigh's nag today?" a foppishly dressed man in a puce coat wanted to know.

"First time on the big course," Richard admitted, grinning.

"Want to bet that Wilborn's Fancy don't beat him?"

"How much?"

"Say, five hundred? Even odds."

"Done." Richard retrieved a slender leather folder from inside his jacket and drew out a sheaf of banknotes. Counting through them, he pulled off the five hundred pounds while Harriet watched in

shocked disbelief. Handing them to another gentleman, he murmured just loud enough for her to hear
him, "You do not mind holding the money, do you?"

The track stewards shouted for the track to be
cleared, and the men melted away. Richard walked
back to the carriage and heaved himself up into the
seat opposite hers.

"You wagered five hundred pounds!"

"Of course I did! You did not think I should come
and not bet, did you?" An infectious grin spread
across his face and crinkled the corners of his eyes.
"Worried that I shall find myself in dun territory,
my dear?"

"Yes."

"Well, I shan't." He leaned across to pat the muff.
" 'Tis but another five hundred we shall have to
split."

"I thought you said that ladies did not sit in the
stands to be ogled by the gentlemen," she observed,
turning her attention to a particularly pretty
woman who clung to a pink of the *ton*.

"They don't usually." His eyes followed her gaze,
and his grin broadened even further. "I collect you
mean that bit of fluff on Chatsworth's arm. Lud,
Harry, how green you are if you have mistaken her
for a lady. That, dear Coz, is naught but a fair
Cyprian."

"Oh. Well, how was I to know that?" she retorted
peevishly.

"You weren't, and I was not supposed to be so
blunt about it. But that is one of the things I like
about you—I've never had to stand on ceremony
with you."

The trumpet sounded, signaling the lineup for the
race, and the woman with the fancy blue hat was
forgotten in the surge of excitement Harriet felt as
the jockey rode Two Harry out to take his place at

the starting gate. The sun caught the shimmer of rose and green satin, and her heart swelled with pride. He rode her horse, and he wore her colors. And then she knew fear.

What if Two Harry lost? What if Richard lost his money? She drew her hand out of the muff and clutched the pull-strap tightly, both afraid to watch and afraid to look away for fear she'd miss the race. She closed her eyes tightly, wishing fervently that Two Harry could somehow win.

"Harry, if you do not look, you will not see, and we will have perjured ourselves for naught."

She felt his warm, strong clasp as his hand covered hers, holding it. "I pray he wins," she managed as she opened her eyes.

"He will."

The starter's pistol fired just then, and the horses surged forward, a blur of bright colors lunging from the gate. At first, Two Harry was but at mid-pack, and Harriet jumped up, bumping her head on the carriage roof.

"Oh, he's got to run—he's got to run! Why doesn't Mr. Ellis do something? Richard!" she screeched.

Just then Two Harry pounded to the outside and gained ground on the leader. "He's running third, Harry—he's running third!" Richard yelled next to her ear.

"Second—he's second!" she shouted back, pounding against the window. "Come on, Two Harry—run!" she screamed, heedless of any who could hear her. "Run!" The leaders were so close rounding the final curve that she couldn't see whether Two Harry led or not, and for a moment it looked as though another horse might overtake the field. "Oh, I cannot watch!" But neither could she look away. And to her amazement, when they thundered into her full view, Two Harry was pulling ahead. "Richard! Richard! I think he is going to win!" she shrieked, tugging on his coat sleeve excitedly.

And as they crossed the finish line, Two Harry led by a good neck. Richard caught Harriet, hugging her jubilantly. "I told you we'd win—I told you!" And then, still holding her so tightly she was breathless, he kissed her full on the mouth. A shiver ran up her spine and she clutched his coat with both hands.

Abruptly he released her, apologizingly, "I'm sorry—I should not have done that. 'Twas the winning." His eyes dancing still, he did not note her stunned expression as he went on, "We won, Harry—can you believe it? We won!"

The jockey still rode Two Harry, slowing first to a canter and then to a walk to cool the animal down. And then he moved to the winner's circle. His face still smiling broadly, Richard jumped down to collect his wager.

It was over so quickly that Harriet thought she must surely have dreamed it, but when he came back, his fist was full of banknotes. "Wilborn's," he announced succinctly as he rejoined her. "We'll collect the race purse later." Then, without warning, he let out another whoop. "I told you we had a winner!"

"I'm so glad."

"Here—count out your half."

"Oh, no. Surely you must have had some expenses—the colors. . . . Mr. Cates and Mr. Ellis, after all."

"You don't want your money?"

"Well, I do not precisely have a use for it just now, Richard, and I cannot simply go home and hide it under the bed."

"Then I'll save it for you." He reached across to

hug her again, but this time he did not kiss her, much to her disappointment. "I owe it all to you, Harry. Without your loan, someone else would've raced him today."

"Fiddle."

"What a strange little creature you are, Coz. I am offering you my undying gratitude, and you will have none of it."

"I don't want gratitude." A rare smile crossed her face and lit her brown eyes. "Besides, we are even—you have my cats."

They stayed through two more races, waiting for the results of Two Harry's win to be made official, and then Richard reluctantly decided that it was time to leave if they were to call on Mrs. Thornton and reach Rowe's Hill with none the wiser. To celebrate, he stopped at an inn and procured a light nuncheon in a basket to be eaten on the way back. And as the carriage lurched forward again, he produced a bottle of wine.

"Oh, I could not," she protested. "Whatever should Mrs. Thornton think if I were to arrive disguised?"

"One glass—I'd share a toast."

"I . . . I cannot . . . I dare not."

"Dare, Harry. One glass is scarce enough to make you bosky at all."

"No." And then, to change the subject, she looked out the window. "It was a splendid adventure, you know—splendid. I shall treasure it for the rest of my life."

"Maybe we can do it again," he offered.

"It is enough that we did not get caught this once."

The drive in front of the Thornton house was empty, and there did not appear to be anyone at home when they arrived. But thinking that perhaps

the Reverend Mr. Thornton had taken the carriage
to pay calls amongst his parish, Harriet insisted
they stop anyway. To her surprise, it was the vicar
himself who answered the door. And his surprise
was as evident as hers.

"Oh, my dear Miss Rowe! And Lord Sherborne!
I fear you are come all this way for naught."

"Oh. Yes, well, do tell Mrs. Thornton I called."

"There's no need for that, my dear—you may tell
her yourself."

"I beg your pardon?"

"She was driving out anyway, so she thought to
stop by Rowe's Hill today to discuss bridal plans."

Harriet's face was blank for a moment as she
digested this unwelcome bit of news, and then she
groaned. "Oh, dear . . . oh, no!"

"I say, is anything amiss, my dear?"

"Oh, no . . . no, of course not," she managed.

"Tell her not to tarry overlong, will you? We are
promised to the Marches for supper," he called
after her as she turned back to Sherborne's
carriage.

"Lud!" Richard muttered succinctly as he handed
her up once again. "I'd say we're in the basket."

She swallowed hard and nodded. "I think I shall
take some wine after all, if you do not mind
terribly."

"I cannot take you home disguised," he told her,
uncorking the bottle. "And you'd best watch out—
too much and you will shoot the cat."

"I think I am going to be sick anyway."

"Then you do not need any of this." Nonetheless,
he poured her a little into a small metal cup and
handed it over. For himself, he reserved the rest of
the bottle.

8 "Buck up, Harry," Richard said encouragingly as they halted in front of Rowe's Hill. "They cannot, after all, eat you."

But she was not attending. Her eyes were fixed on the carriage parked ahead of them, and her face bore a totally stricken look. It was going to be deuced unpleasant, and they both knew it.

"Harry, I won't let them punish you—'twas my fault in the first place."

"No."

He slid down and reached up to help her. Her hand was as ice in his as she stepped from the carriage, and she shivered. "Harry . . ." he began helplessly.

Her chin shot up as she straightened her back resolutely, and a deep sigh escaped her. "No, you are quite right: she cannot do more to me than she has already done, I think."

"That's the ticket."

"But do you mind terribly if I hang on to your arm just now?"

"Not at all."

Silence greeted them, a pregnant silence that boded ill for Harriet, as they entered the front saloon. Mrs. Thornton's teacup was suspended halfway to her lips, and Hannah Rowe's countenance was frozen into a mask of outrage. Only Sir

John moved, and when he did, it was to rise from his chair to advance on them. Richard could feel Harriet's fingers clutch his sleeve convulsively, as though she feared to be struck. Instinctively he stepped in front of her to shield her from her father's wrath.

"Well, missy, what have you to say for yourself?" Sir John demanded. Then, not waiting for her to answer, he looked up at Richard. "As for you, sirrah, I shall speak with you privately later!"

"No," Harriet managed almost inaudibly, humiliated that he should speak so in front of the vicar's wife. If her own father would act as though she'd committed an indiscretion publicly, 'twas certain to be spread about the neighborhood. "Papa, 'tis not—"

"There is but one reason for prevarication of this sort, missy, and I shudder to think . . . to admit that a daughter of mine would seek to deceive me so!"

"Uh . . ." Mrs. Thornton's teacup clattered against her saucer as she rose hastily. "Really, but I should be on my way now that she is found safe after all." Casting a disapproving glance at Harriet, she added ominously, "But what Edwin is to think of this, I am sure I do not know."

"Uncle, if I could be private with you for a moment *now*," Richard murmured significantly.

"Harriet, you will retire to your chamber," Hannah told her coldly. "Your papa and I will attend to you later, miss."

"No! I am not a child to be sent to bed, Mama. I do not know what you think, but—"

"Harriet!" her father thundered, raising his hand.

"Stop it, all of you! The fault is not hers," Richard heard himself say. Then, as they all looked at him, he nodded. "As I said, if you will but attend me privately, both of you, I think we may resolve the matter."

"Richard—"

"No, Harry, the fault *was* mine, after all. 'Tis up to me to satisfy your parents. If you will but see Mrs. Thornton out and wait for me, we shall come about, I promise."

She looked from him to Hannah and her father, and despite her earlier resolve to face them, she hesitated. "Just so, Harry," Richard told her gently. "You have naught to fear—wait upstairs."

"But . . ."

His blue eyes met hers and held. "Please."

There was such kindness there that she had to look away. Dropping her eyes and feeling very much the coward, she bobbed her head in assent. "All right."

As her parents withdrew into her father's library, she was left to follow a very rigid Mrs. Thornton into the outer hall. There seemed to be no explanation that would not further outrage that lady, so she remained silent whilst Thomas assisted her into her pelisse. Drawing on her gloves, Mrs. Thornton finally spoke.

"I trust you will have a suitable explanation for my son."

Harriet's chin came up at the censorious tone in the older woman's voice. "I did but attend the races, ma'am, and I see nothing so remiss in that."

"Humph! We shall see, Miss Rowe—we shall see. But then, I expect one lie to breed another, after all. Just remember—'tis not I whom you must satisfy, but rather Edwin."

With that cryptic remark, Edwin's mother departed. Harriet stood in the doorway watching her drive out of sight, feeling oddly relieved. As much as her parents would be vexed with her, they would have to accept it when Edwin Thornton cried off. And, given his extremely narrow sense of propriety, it was almost certain that he would.

As she finally climbed the stairs to her chamber, she could hear her father shouting and Richard raising his voice in answer. And from time to time Hannah joined in to defend her nephew and condemn Harriet. It was an unpleasant interview, one that was growing more rancorous by the moment, but by the sound of it, Richard was more than holding his own. She could hear the words "unnatural parent" uttered more than once.

Throwing herself on her bed in her chilly room, Harriet waited for the quarrel belowstairs to end. She ought not to be such a coward, she told herself severely; she ought to be down there defending herself. But somehow she had not the will to listen to Hannah—not today. Today. She sat up and pulled the coverlet up around her, shutting out the noise, remembering instead the glorious adventure of going to Newmarket, of seeing her horse win. No matter what the punishment, it would be worth those few hours of freedom, those few hours shared with Richard Standen.

It was some time before there was a knock at the door, and her heart lay like a rock in her breast at the thought of facing Hannah again. She swallowed hard, not answering.

"Harry . . ."

She was unprepared for the sound of his voice. Her eyes widened as the door creaked open and he stepped inside. But the look on his face sent a chill of apprehension coursing through her.

"I expected Hannah," she offered lamely, rising to sit on the edge of the bed.

"You ought to have a fire—you'll take a chill."

"I know, but 'tis a waste of wood."

"Harry, I'm sorry for this. I would not . . . I should not have taken you."

"No. 'Tis not your fault. I wanted to go."

He stood there, hesitating for a moment, and then he sat down beside her. "Aunt Hannah would have it that Mr. Thornton will cry off, Harry."

"Then not all is lost, is it?"

"Yes. Yes, it is, and I am sorry for it. By nightfall, Mrs. Thornton will have told the Marches, and before sunset tomorrow, 'twill be the *on-dit* of East Anglia, I fear."

"As if I cared a fig for that."

Again there was a hesitation, and he inhaled sharply, looking away. "Harry, I know I am not the sort of husband you would have, but there's no help for it—you'll have to take me."

The room spun around her. She stared blankly, trying to assimilate what he'd said, and then she blinked as though that could somehow clear her head. "*What?*" she gasped.

"I said Edwin Thornton is going to cry off, and you'll have to wed me to avoid the scandal."

It was not the proposal of her dreams—it was not even a proposal. His blue eyes were sober as they met hers, his face as somber as though he'd told her somebody had died. It was rich, the tricks that fate played on one, she thought as she searched his handsome face. Her foolish dreams had borne bitter fruit, for the man she loved offered for her out of pity.

"No."

"Harry, think."

A deep sigh escaped her, taking with it the hope of years. "I have," she answered simply, "and I cannot ask you to do it."

"Do not be a fool, Harry."

"No."

Her resolve surprised him. "Hannah and your father will not stand with you, you know. Ten to one, they have already convinced Mrs. Thornton you are hopelessly compromised."

"It doesn't matter."

"Harry . . ."

She rose from the bed and backed away from the temptation to take his offer. "You cannot pretend any affection for me, can you? You cannot truly say you wish to wed me! There is not that between us!" she cried in anguish. "Do not make me say no again, I beg of you!"

"Whether I wish to wed you or not is nothing to the point, Harry! I pray you will not be getting missish with me—this is Richard, you know!"

"*Do* you wish to marry me?"

"No! Of course not! But I'll not see you ruined either—I'll not have that laid on my head, thank you!"

"Then leave! I shall not lay it on your head, after all—and I am the one who counts!" She choked as tears of anger and hurt welled in her eyes and threatened to betray her. "I see no reason why you must pay for that which never happened."

"Coming it too strong, Harry! Dash it, you know what is expected of both of us, and—"

"Just go, Richard." Her voice dropped miserably. "Tell them that I have refused your suit."

He reached out a hand to her, but she backed further away. "Please, Richard," she whispered.

"Harry, I'm sorry—truly I would not have wished this for the world."

"I know." She wrenched open the door and clung to the edge of it. "You must not think I do not thank you for the offer."

There was no help for it then. Clearly he'd overset her terribly. " 'Twill not be pleasant for you, I fear," he told her as he stepped past her.

"It never is."

He walked down the steps slowly, thinking he ought to feel relieved that she'd rejected his reluctant suit. But somehow he felt more guilty than anything. Even at twenty-four, she was but a green girl, while he ought to have known better. His aunt and uncle were waiting for him when he reached the bottom.

"She would not have me," he announced simply, passing them.

For a moment Hannah stared after him, stunned. Sir John choked apoplectically, seeing not Richard Standen, but rather the extremely wealthy Viscount Sherborne, and when he found his voice, he sputtered, "Wouldn't have you? What nonsense is this? She *has* to take you! Dash it, sirrah, but she must! 'Twill be all over the neighborhood when Thornton refuses her!"

Richard turned back briefly, his disgust written on his face. "No. No, she does not. You forget she is a woman grown, Uncle."

"Wait! Where are you going?"

"To see to Two Harry—to see to my horse. He won today, you know. And to see Thornton when he returns home—'tis the least I can do for her."

"Egad."

"But you will be back?" Hannah wanted to know.

"For tonight only." His eyes met hers in warning. "Do not be harsh with her—at least until you know what Thornton means to do."

The door closed behind him, leaving both of them at a loss as to what to do. Hannah, who'd not really wanted to see her vexatious stepdaughter become a viscountess anyway, muttered that she certainly hoped he would persuade Thornton of the innocence of the situation.

"Humph! So the beast won, did he?" her husband snorted, considering the unpleasantness over for the moment at least. "Two Harry! What the devil sort of name is that for a horse, I ask you?"

"He probably named the animal for his father and himself," Hannah responded dryly, disappointed that Sir John could be diverted from the matter so easily.

Harriet lay staring at the ceiling, listening to the sound of Richard's carriage leaving the drive. It was probably the last time she would see him for a long time, she reflected morosely. And it was never, never going to be the same between them, for her dreams were dashed on the shores of reality. He'd offered for her out of pity.

She did not even pay any attention when Hannah opened her door. The older woman surveyed her coldly, her gaze taking in the red puffiness around Harriet's eyes.

"Well, missy," her stepmama snapped finally, " 'tis a fine broth you have brewed yourself!"

"Yes. Yes, it is, Mama." She sat up, meeting those cold, narrow eyes squarely. "But I do not repine, after all, for it must surely rid me of Mr. Thornton."

9 Choosing to eat in her room rather than endure any further harassment from either Hannah or her father, Harriet sat before the small fire she'd kindled and polished off the last of the cold mutton Thomas had slipped her. That she could not endure living at Rowe's Hill for the rest of her life was abundantly clear to her. She had to escape, and soon. Why, oh why, had Plimly not answered? Surely the nurse who'd cared for her so lovingly in childhood cared for her still. But it was well over two months since she'd sent her first letter. And even if Hannah had intercepted it, it did not explain the others. She had Thomas' word that he'd posted the last one in the village himself.

She was surely the most miserable of creatures, the most spineless, dejected female alive. And now she'd even lost the only relative she could call a friend, for it was not likely that he would wish to come to Rowe's Hill again.

"Harriet! Harriet! Thomas, you will fetch Miss Rowe on the instant, if you please."

It was Hannah, and from the sound of her voice, she was no longer angry, no longer angry at all. And then Harriet, who'd been so absorbed in her own dejection, realized that there was someone else there, for her ears picked up the buzz of conversation between her father and another man. She rose from her chair cautiously, laying aside the napkin that had covered her lap.

She paused in the doorway to listen, and the awful suspicion that it was Edwin washed over her. Her fears were confirmed when Thomas met her as she stepped into the hall.

"You have a caller, miss—'tis Mr. Thornton, just arrived from the village."

Momentary panic assailed her. Surely he must have heard of her escapade . . . surely he must wish to cry off—he must. But Hannah did not sound vexed, and that did not augur well.

"Oh, dear." Well, there was but one way to discover for certain, after all. She sucked in her breath, letting it out slowly to compose her disordered thoughts. Then, lifting her head and squaring her shoulders in preparation for the unpleasantness, she nodded. "You may tell Mr. Thornton I shall be down forthwith, Thomas."

It was certain to be an unpleasant interview, yet when she entered the front saloon, she was not at all displeased to discover that her father and Hannah had deserted her. Instead, she faced Edwin Thornton alone, prepared to endure his censure as a small price to pay for an end to their betrothal. He was standing with his back to her when she entered the room, his attention focused on the Ormolu clock on the mantel.

"Well, you are prompt at least," he observed, turning around. Then, without further preamble, he cleared his throat and began. "I came as soon as I was apprised of the situation, Harriet, and though I am sorely displeased by what you have done, I would not have you think I mean to desert you."

It was the second time within the space of seven hours that she had been completely stunned. "You mean you are not going to cry off?" she uttered faintly, blinking in shock. "Oh, but you must!"

It was as though she hadn't spoken. He merely continued in the same vein, saying, "While I cannot condone that you have misled your parents or that you have been present at what I can only describe as a completely unfit place for a lady—"

"It was Newmarket," she injected tiredly. "And I was far from the only female present. Moreover, I was in the company of my cousin, sir."

"It was a horsetrack, Miss Rowe! A sporting place!"

"Yes," she admitted mildly, "and I enjoyed it excessively."

"Naturally, you cannot know of what you speak, Harriet. But I quite fault Sherborne as much as you, though I admit that before he explained it all to me, I was not certain I could excuse what I can only consider reprehensible behavior."

"Sher . . . Richard spoke to you, sir?" she demanded incredulously. "*Why?*"

"Well, naturally he expected some unpleasant gossip over the matter, I should think, and he wished me to know that the blame was not yours alone. And while I am still by no means pleased, I will own that you have not much experience before the world, Harriet."

"He should not have come to you."

"My dear, as your betrothed, I had the right to an explanation. But you must not think all is lost," he added pompously, "for I mean to support you publicly in this. However, I take leave to tell you privately that I shall not tolerate any further misconduct. I shall not allow your name to be bandied about further, whatever the circumstances, and I think it best that you not be seen again with Sherborne ere we are wed."

"I have no intention—"

"Moreover, I think it best that we understand each other completely, my dear. While I shall stand beside you through the unpleasant gossip, you will conduct yourself with the circumspection I should naturally expect in a wife. You have clearly shown that you are in need of my guidance in all things, and I should expect that upon our marriage, you will allow that I am to control your property as well as your person."

"By that I collect you mean my mother's portion?" she asked with deceptive sweetness.

"But of course."

"Alas, but I cannot."

"But two thousand pounds is too—"

"—much for a female?" she finished for him. "Well, it is mine, sir—mine."

The firmness in her voice surprised and irritated him. "I think you mistake the matter, Harriet, for the choice is no longer yours. If you would have my support—"

"No, sir, I would not."

"But—"

"And Richard had no right to explain anything to you. In short, Mr. Thornton, I find myself unable to continue this sham of a betrothal between us."

It was his turn to stare blankly, and then his face reddened as he perceived she meant it. She faced him determinedly, her face set, her hands clenched.

"You cannot mean it."

It surprised her that she'd actually said it, but the relief she felt more than compensated for anything that Hannah could do to her. "Yes," she answered quite simply, "I do. We should not suit."

"Then you must be prepared for the sort of gossip that will come from this," he told her nastily, "for 'twill be said that I am discarding you, you know."

"As I do not go about much, I should not expect that to weigh heavily."

"And do not be expecting Sherborne to come up to scratch."

"I assure you I do not."

He stared at her as though seeing her for the first time, not so much as he had thought her, but rather as she was. Clearly she was not worthy of the honor he'd once thought to bestow on her.

"Very well, then," he managed stiffly. "I can quite see I was mistaken in you, and I can only thank fate that 'twas discovered before I came to regret my regard more bitterly than I do now."

"I am sorry."

"Sorry? Well, I am not! I can quite see that I have been deceived in you, Miss Rowe!" Having for once run out of words, he cast about for his hat, retrieving it from a side table. "You may tell your father I have withdrawn my offer!" Jamming the beaver on his head, he made a hasty exit.

As the front door banged shut after him, her father appeared from around the corner. "Damme, girl! What the devil do you think you are about, anyway? You have made yourself the laughingstock of the neighborhood!"

"I don't care, Papa—I don't care! Do you hear that? I'm not wedding Edwin Thornton, and I am glad of it!"

"Here now, missy! You'll not talk to your papa like that! Not in this house, you won't!" But she'd already brushed past him and was halfway up the stairs. "You come back here, missy! Hannah! Hannah! The silly chit's whistled Thornton down the wind!"

Upstairs, she could hear him calling, his voice growing angrier each time he shouted her name. She shut the door and leaned against it, shaking from the realization of what she'd just done. And for once Hannah did not come up to read a peal over her. Slowly her racng pulse quieted, and with that came the realization that she'd not only broken her betrothal to Edwin but also openly defied her father.

She sank into the chair before the remnants of her cold food and contemplated what must be done. And once again she acutely missed the comfort of her cat. If Athena had been there, she'd have fussed and purred to lighten her mistress's mood. But Hannah had taken her cats as surely as if she had actually drowned them. No, the only comfort she could expect was her own. And hopefully Miss Plimly's.

Much later, she heard Richard's carriage return, long after the household had retired, and she made up her mind. Slipping noiselessly down the back stairs, she met him as he came in. He paused at the sight of her.

"You had not the right to send Edwin over here."

"He came? I was afraid he would not."

"He came because he did not wish to part with his notion of me, and because he had hopes of my portion, if you want the truth of it."

"Harry—"

"No. I know you think you did the right thing, but it would not serve. Wait—" She raised her hand to still him when he started to protest. "I did not come down to quarrel over him. I came to ask for my half of the money."

"What I owe you for Two Harry?"

"No, no, of course not. I still want to think I own half of him, Richard, but I would like to have my portion of what he won today."

Without hesitation he reached beneath his coat and drew out the leather folder swollen with banknotes. And in the dim light of the hall sconces he carefully counted out two hundred and fifty pounds. "There's still the purse, but I have not collected it yet. If you need it, you may have the rest of what we won from Wilborn."

"No."

"Harry, you aren't thinking to do anything foolish, are you?"

"No."

"Well, 'tis yours, in any event." He stood there surveying her awkwardly, thinking there ought to be something else he could do. Finally, when she said nothing more, he nodded. "I expect I shall be leaving tomorrow afternoon, but I will collect the purse first and bring your share back to you ere I go. Next week, I mean to register Two Harry for the overnights at Doncaster, and I'll send you whatever is won there. Or if you prefer it, I can have it placed in your London account."

"Send it to London."

"Harry . . ." He tried to fathom her expression in the faint light, but her face was in deep shadows. "Harry, is aught amiss—other than Hannah and Thornton, I mean?"

"No, naught's amiss, Richard. Just continue caring for my cats, I pray you."

Then, before he realized she meant to leave him standing there, she was up the back stairs. Her footsteps sounded softly on the carpet above him, and then her door closed quietly. It must have been far worse than he'd expected even, and she had no wish to tell him of it. The exhilaration of winning was gone completely, lost somewhere in her dark eyes. Well, she would come about, he decided finally. She was, after all, not a child anymore.

In the quiet of her room, she began packing her two new dresses into her mother's old portmanteau,

stopping only once to listen to him close the door
at the other end of the hall. Everything was amiss,
she thought rebelliously, but she'd get over it. She'd
leave Rowe's Hill and her foolish passion for
Richard Standen behind. Lack of invitation notwith-
standing, she was going to Bath.

10 Harriet debated as to the wisdom of hiring a hackney, but the posting-house attendant had assured her that 'twas not far to the address Plimly had given her. Besides, after suffering the unwelcome attentions of two rather inebriated fellows (for she could not call them gentlemen) on the first leg of her journey and then the rather overwhelming odor of a stout lout and his toothless mother for the last portion, she was ready for the open air. She stopped on the street corner and tried to remember the directions she'd been given.

It must surely be up there, but the narrow lane did not look the least promising, for the lodgings were cramped and close, one upon the other, and the area was quite noisy compared to the quiet of Rowe's Hill. She drew Plimly's last letter, a missive almost a year old, from her reticule and looked at it again.

"Lost, miss?"

She turned around gratefully to discover a man who was by his clothing a gentleman and by his manner not. His eyes traveled insolently over her, taking in the battered bag she'd set down beside her, giving her pause. Resolutely she folded the letter and straightened her shoulders.

"No. I am but visiting an old friend up there."

His eyebrows rose, and he looked at her again, this time with considerably more curiosity. "Up there? Betsy's perhaps?"

"Who?"

"Do not be coming the innocent with me, my dear," he answered, reaching to touch her shoulder with encroaching familiarity as he spoke. When she flinched, his hand slid down her arm, closing roughly on her wrist.

"I assure you you are mistaken, sir," she managed coldly, her pulses racing with sudden fear.

"Oh? I see no abigail or maid," he gibed, tightening his grip.

"You will unhand me this instant." Her voice was even, but her throat was tight. "Otherwise, I shall scream."

His laugh was unpleasant, frightening her even more, and his other hand came up as though he meant to cover her mouth. She bobbed her head, sinking her teeth hard into the fleshy part between his thumb and first finger.

"Ouch, you little vixen!"

"I am being abducted! I am being abducted!" she shouted loudly, pulling away. "I pray someone will help me!"

A door flew open behind her, and a woman with a broom came out in full fury, swinging at Harriet's tormentor, catching him hard in the back of the head. And those who'd been ignoring her before rushed to her aid, abusing him with language she'd never heard in her life. He turned her loose and beat a hasty retreat toward a phaeton at the end of the street, followed by several men all too ready to attack one whose clothes were finer than theirs.

"Well, now, dearie, ain't yer a fine one," the woman observed as she stood staring at Harriet with her elbows akimbo and her hands and broom on her hips. "Betsy's gettin' 'em greener every day, by the looks o' yer."

"I beg your pardon?"

"Ye was goin' up there, wasn't yer?"

"I am looking for Miss Plimly—Miss Violet Plimly—my old nurse from home, and that gentle-man—"

"Nurse! Ain't no nurses there!" the woman snorted.

"Then I was given the wrong direction, for I was told—"

"Must've turned wrong if yer don't belong over here. Nurse!" she exploded derisively.

"Please . . ." Harriet took out the letter again and then looked up at the name written on the side of the corner house. "Yes—'tis the wrong street. Nonetheless, I thank you for your prompt assistance."

"Even talk like the Quality, don't yer? Well, be off with yer ere he comes around again, 'cause Old Peg ain't comin' out but once, yer hear? Aye, wouldn't have then," she grumbled, "but even a whore ought to choose her business."

"A what? Oh, I assure you—"

"That you ain't one o' them? It don't matter anyways. But if ye don't want ter be fondled, yer ought not be alone, yer hear?"

With that bit of advice the woman backed into the narrow house and slammed the door. Harriet stood there feeling like the greenest female on earth, while the sounds of the crowd faded into the next street. She retraced her steps nervously, walking as fast as the portmanteau would allow, until she reached the posting house from whence she'd come, vowing to hire a hackney or a sedan chair after all.

But the results, while not nearly so dramatic, were little better. As she was set down in front of a tall, narrow house quite away from any of the fashionable crescents, or so the driver had told her with a sniff, it appeared the place was deserted. The upper windows were shuttered despite the mildness of the spring day, and the curtains were closed below. With real trepidation she knocked, timidly at first, then with both hands balled into fists.

And the awful suspicion that she'd run away to Bath for naught crept into her mind. She was alone in Bath with no maid and no acquaintance. But she did have nearly two hundred and fifty pounds, she reminded herself in an effort to lift her flagging spirits. And she could not go back—no matter what she did, she could not go back. 'Twould be easier to hire a maid and set up some sort of shop than face Hannah again.

Just as she'd quite given up, the inner latch was lifted and the door opened a crack, revealing quite an elderly lady in a mobcap and apron. "Here, now, there's no need to bring the house down on my ears just because they are not what they used to be, is there?"

"I am seeking Miss Plimly—Miss Violet Plimly," Harriet announced loudly.

"Eh? Oh, you are come to see Letty?" The door opened a little wider. "She's gone."

"Gone? Oh, no! Oh, dear. Where?"

"Heart quit, or so 'twas thought by Dr. Wilkes."

"Her heart quit?" Harriet had to lean against the wall for support, managing feebly, "You mean . . . ?"

"It came on her so quickly." The old woman's voice quavered as she spoke. "We'd just come from church when she said she did not feel quite the thing, you see. I went to brew her a cup of tea, and when I came back, she was lying on the floor." She dabbed at her eyes with a corner of her apron. "Oh, dear, how I do go on."

Harriet's throat constricted as she felt the very real pain of loss. Plimly had died, and Harriet had not even known of it. And the lowering thought that she had made her plans long after the old nurse was gone somehow made it worse. She ought to have been there, she ought to have known. "Oh, I wrote to her," she said lamely.

"And I meant to answer, my dear, but these eyes fail me, and I could not bring myself to ask a stranger to do it. I do miss her terribly." Dabbing at pale, rheumy eyes, she shook her head. "But I daresay we shall meet again, do you not think?" Then, peering more closely at Harriet, she decided, "Oh, but you must be Letty's Miss Rowe?"

"Yes. And you must be Miss Agnes."

The white cap bobbed in acknowledgement. "I was the elder, you know. Well, she would have liked to see you, I know. Spoke of you often, she did." Then, recalling her manners, she moved back from the door. "Guess you'd wish to come in, wouldn't you? Might as well have some tea with me ere you go back, after all. Just wish I'd written, but I was waiting for Philip to come—I thought perhaps he would tend to the matter for me."

Motioning Harriet in after her, she gestured to a small room. "It ain't much, is it? But I hate to leave it, you know. Always thought she'd outlive me, being younger and all, and I'd not have to do this. Daresay there's not much to count on in this world, is there?"

There were packing boxes piled neatly along one wall, and two trunks stood at the end of a thread-worn settee. The small woman fretted about the room, searching in one of the crates for something.

"Do sit down, Miss Rowe. I shall find the good napkins directly." Then, straightening in triumph, she smoothed two white linen squares with her wrinkled hands.

"Philip's coming—Friday, he said." The pale eyes rested on the younger woman's face. " 'Tis Thursday today, isn't it? Well, I'm going to live with him. Daresay I won't like it, but I do not mean to be found here one day, gone like Letty. A person wants relations around when it happens, you know."

"Yes, of course, and you should," Harriet assured her, taking a seat on the faded settee. But even as she sat down, she realized she was truly at point nonplus. "I do not suppose you would wish to stay here, would you?" she asked, trying not to sound desperate. "I mean, I could remain for a while if you should wish it."

"Of course I would stay! But I have accepted that I cannot, and Philip's my blood—got no other now. Besides, I got no money left either." Agnes Plimly's veined hands shook as she took out two china cups. "Letty must've told you of him, I should think. Only nephew, you know, and since his Rose is gone also, 'tis best for both of us."

The old woman rattled on, heedless of Harriet's distress, but Harriet was no longer attending fully. Her beloved Miss Plimly was gone, she'd run away for naught, and now she truly had nowhere to go. There was George, of course, but she had not the least notion of where to look for him, and it was doubtful that he'd wish to be burdened with a spinster sister, after all.

"You are welcome to stay with me until he comes," she heard Agnes Plimly tell her. "There's still Letty's bed, and I should be grateful of the company. 'Tis tedious, being alone before the world, my dear, and Letty did speak so often of you that I quite feel I know you. But of course if you've no wish to be burdened with a crotchety old woman, I could quite understand."

"I should like very much to stay," Harriet answered sincerely. "If it does not distress you overmuch, I'd like to speak of her—she was so very dear to me."

"Of course she was." Agnes wiped a spilling tear from her eyes again, and began pouring tea. "I hope you do not mind too much, but these leaves are not fresh, although I have used them but once before. Economy, you know. When one gets old, one must be ever so careful of one's small savings."

Harriet remembered then that Plimly had told her that Agnes had not been so fortunate as she was, and had served as a dresser to one of Bath's shabby genteel families for years. "But surely your employer pensioned you," she suggested.

"Oh, she gave me what she could afford, I suppose, but 'twas not nearly enough. And I cannot say that Lady Rowe was particularly generous with Letty either—but I shall not speak of that."

"My stepmother is not generous to any, I fear." Harriet moved the reticule she'd set beside her and felt the roll of banknotes inside. Impulsively she leaned forward. "Actually, I am terribly sorry that I did not see Miss Plimly .... before ...."

". . . she passed on? Oh, I assure you that she did not fault you for it," Agnes hastened to reassure her. "And she did treasure your letters. I have heard every one a dozen times, I vow."

"Yes, but I have some money that belonged to her. I . . . I dared not send it lest Hannah—Lady Rowe— find out, and . . . well, of course, I can quite see that it must be yours now."

"Letty left some money?" The old woman's eyes

brightened and her veined hands shook as she poured more of the pale tea. "Oh, I did not know . . . I had no notion . . ."

" 'Twas not much," Harriet invented, calculating rapidly just how much she could afford to spare. " 'Twas but fifty pounds."

"*Fifty* pounds!" Agnes looked faint.

"Had it been more, I should have pushed to send it earlier."

"More? Oh, my dear Miss Rowe, 'tis a year and more of what I was used to earn! Oh, my!" She repossessed the teacup from Harriet's hand. "I should say fresh tea is in order for this. Fifty pounds! Oh, but then 'twas Letty's, and I—"

"I am certain she would wish you to have it."

"And you have traveled all this way to deliver it. Oh, my dear, but you are all Letty said of you."

"Actually, I have run away from my home—I have not so much as a maid with me," Harriet announced with a baldness that astounded even her. "And I thought to bring Plimly the money and ask if 'twere possible for me to live with her."

"She would have welcomed you, but—"

"I know. When I was a child, we often spoke of setting up a house here," Harriet admitted wistfully. "I'd hoped it were yet possible, but I can see . . ."

"Well, if Philip were not coming, I should welcome you, of course. But Philip is alone also, and I—"

"Oh, I should not expect it now. I can see 'twould not serve."

The old woman sighed as she sat down again and began pouring the stronger tea. "Well, I could ask Philip," she began irresolutely, "but his house is as small as this one."

"No. No, I pray you will not."

"But what will you do? A female cannot live alone, and you are scarce fit for dressing or being a lady's maid—not one as gently bred as you, my dear. And you would not wish to be a lady's companion, I can tell you, for you are not treated as any but poor relation. 'Tis a pity you did not marry."

"I have my own competence."

"But your papa—"

"My father has no control over it. The thing of the matter is," Harriet admitted candidly, "I have not the least notion of what to do with it."

"Well, I daresay we shall think of something," Agnes murmured doubtfully.

A loud pounding sounded on the outer door, intensifying as the old woman gave a nervous start. "Oh, dear," she gasped in consternation. "You do not suppose I misunderstood and he said Thursday, do you?" Setting her teacup aside, she rose to answer the door. "I am coming, Philip!" she called out.

Harriet's back was to the door, but her heart gave a leap as she heard him ask, "Your pardon, but is there a Miss Harriet Rowe here?"

"Richard!" She spun around, oversetting the cup that had been balanced on her knee. "Oh, dear! That is . . . How did you ever find me?"

She did not know whether it was the rush of gratitude she felt on seeing him, or whether it was really so, but just then he was the handsomest man she'd ever seen—ever. He stepped through the door, filling it, removing his hat from his disordered, windblown black hair. But his face was grim, almost angry, when he faced her.

" 'Tis a devil of a chase you've led me, Harry!" he complained. And then, seeing her pleasure fade to guilt, he reached to catch her hands in his gloved ones. " 'Gad, Harry, but you gave me a fright, girl. When I returned with your share of the purse, Aunt Hannah greeted me with the news that you had fled. And nigh the breadth of England! Had she not recalled your Miss Plimly, I'd not have known where to look."

"I could not stay." She twisted her hands in his and looked away before daring again to meet his gaze. "I swear I could not."

"I know." His voice softened, and his blue eyes bore into hers. "But it won't serve. A female alone cannot survive, Harry—certainly not a green girl such as you. You know that, do you not?"

"I . . . I came to live with Plimly, Richard, but she . . ."

"No." His fingers massaged hers as he held them. "You are going to have to take me, Harry. I am the best choice you have."

Her eyes widened, taking in the soberness of his, and her heart beat rapidly at the feel of his strong hands on hers. There was no questioning that he was right, or that he was the man she wanted. And her mind told her that if he had journeyed all the way to Bath after her, he must have some regard for her, after all.

"Well, Harry?"

And at that moment, in her foolish heart, she dared to dream that she could make him love her. This time, she nodded.

And if he did not look precisely overjoyed, neither did he appear unhappy. He released one of her hands to brush at a tendril of hair that had escaped to fall forward over her brow. "I shall try to be a good husband to you, Harry—I promise you that. We are in no worse case than full half the *ton*, after all."

Agnes Plimly looked from one to the other of them, her old face confused. "I say . . ."

"Uh . . ." Reddening in embarrassment, Harriet moved self-consciously to his side. "Oh, you must be wondering . . ."

"Richard Standen—Sherborne, actually— Harriet's betrothed," he answered for her, extending his hand.

11 It was agreed, since she'd brought no maid or abigail, that the wisest course would be to marry immediately, return to Rowe's Hill to collect whatever she required of her meager possessions, and then press on to Richlands. There she would remain, mastering the running of her new household whilst he took Two Harry to Doncaster. To Harriet it was as though she were in a dream from which she hoped she never wakened.

After sharing tea with Agnes Plimly, Richard propelled his betrothed to his carriage, saying they must hurry if they were to avail themselves of the special license he'd brought with him that day. Thus it was that Harriet found herself in the parlor of the rector of St. Michael's and St. Paul's Church in Bath, listening to Richard explain the need for speedy nuptials. The words were spoken, the ring he usually wore on his little finger was slipped on hers, and the marriage lines duly witnessed. By dusk she was lawfully Harriet Rowe Standen, Viscountess Sherborne.

"I had thought to break our journey at the Black Lion Inn some fifteen miles from here," he told her as he handed her up into his carriage. "Unless, of course, you should wish otherwise."

She had to blink back tears, for never in fourteen years and more had she been asked rather than told what she would do. " 'Twill be fine," she managed, settling into the seat across from him. "Oh, 'tis ever so much more comfortable here than in the mail coach."

"I should hope so. What the devil were you thinking of, my dear? You could have been molested—or worse, you know."

"So I discovered," she admitted ruefully.

"Thing is, I don't see how you managed to leave Rowe's Hill without being detected. I mean, 'tis not as though it were in town."

"Well . . . I do not suppose you would tell Hannah of it anyway, would you? No, of course you would not," she decided. " 'Twas Thomas. I persuaded him to hire his brother, who is in Squire March's employ, for he often goes into the village in the cart. Thomas took my portmanteau when he rode over to engage him, and then I walked across the back fields to the next lane, where, for the princely sum of ten pounds, I was met the next morning. I caught the mail coach in Cambridge, transferred in Wallingford, and arrived here today. It was not, I fear, a very comfortable journey, for I could scarce sleep."

"Well, you will never have to face such an ordeal again, Harry, for I mean to take care of you."

He spoke as though he thought of her as a helpless child, she thought, and while his words were meant to comfort, they did not satisfy that in her which wished desperately for his love. But aloud she said, " 'Tis to be hoped we shall take care of each other, isn't it?"

He could not fail to note the wistfulness in her voice, and he leaned across, covering her folded hands with his. "Of course it is, my dear. And you must not think I am repining over this marriage."

"Yes, well, I know I am not what you would have

chosen for your viscountess, Richard, so there is no need to—"

"Harry . . . Harry . . . you must not think I had romantical notions about my marriage. If I have any regrets, 'tis only that I had not wanted to wed so soon."

She wanted to believe him more than anything, but she could not resist asking, "But did you not wish for an Incomparable?"

"I suppose every man dreams of an Incomparable. But I daresay Incomparables may not in fact make the best wives, when all is said and done. I want a comfortable wife, Harry, a woman to listen to me, to rear my children."

"Oh."

"I do want children, Harry. My parents had but me, for I am told they did not rub together at all well, and I always felt the lack." He leaned back then, stretching his long legs as best he could within the confines of the coach, and surveyed her lazily from beneath lashes so black they looked like coal smudges against his face. "You do not look twenty-four at all," he decided.

She reached up self-consciously to smooth back the stray hairs that insisted on falling over her forehead and at her temples. "Well, I suppose if I wore it down I might look a trifle younger."

"You mistake me. I meant you look much younger now."

"I do?"

His gaze dropped lower, straying speculatively from her shoulders to her waist. With a start, she realized he'd never looked quite that way at her before.

"You know, Harry, you are trimmer than I thought."

"Edwin said I was too thin by half."

"Then he did not know what to appreciate in a female. He must surely view women like cattle if he thinks that."

The laziness had crept into his voice, sending a very pleasant shiver through her. Nonplussed, she looked out the window into the darkening countryside. "Yes, well, I should like to forget Mr. Thornton."

She had a very fine profile and very fine eyes. No, she was not a beauty, he admitted to himself, but she would show to advantage once he got her out of those awful dresses Hannah had bought her. But she would never be truly fashionable, for he supposed, for she lacked the social ease so necessary for successful entry into the *ton.* And that did bother him. Before his Uncle John had insisted on this marriage, Richard had always thought that his wife would be elegant, witty, and accomplished. But Harriet had never had the chance to be anything other than a colorless, timid girl, and he could not quite bring himself to fault her for what she could not help. Besides, she was a very good sort of a girl, one usually devoid of feminine wiles, and she ought to make him a more-than-adequate wife. No, he meant to make the best of his unwanted marriage.

As it grew darker inside the carriage, they both lapsed into silence, each lost in his own assessment of what life with the other would bring. And neither spoke again until the coach rolled into the lighted yard of the Black Lion Inn.

"Well, my dear, it looks as though we have arrived," he announced, straightening in his seat.

"Yes."

"Wait here whilst I bespeak a chamber and a private parlor for us."

With that, he'd jumped down, closing the carriage door behind him, leaving her with the realization

he'd said "chamber." She felt the lump of his ring
through her glove and told herself she was a
married lady. And she wondered if she were going
to discover those mysteries Hannah only hinted
darkly at whenever she mentioned the married
state. Well, it could not be so very bad, Harriet
reasoned to still her rising qualms, else how could
it be that so many females wished to be wed?

"Do you wish to refresh yourself before supper?"
Richard asked, wrenching open her door and
reaching for her.

Light and shadow caught his face, transforming
it, and his blue eyes reflected the gold of the lantern
that hung above the door. For a moment she was
scared, and then his strong hands clasped her waist,
lifting her down. His coat sleeve brushed against
the front of her pelisse as he reached for her hand.
And she was so very conscious of how much bigger
than she he was.

"Tired?"

"A little," she lied. In truth, she was exhausted
from a two-and-one-half-day ride in mail coaches
and a long day in Bath.

"So am I. I feel as though I've lived in my carriage
ever since Hannah told me you'd gone." He slipped
her hand into the crook of his arm. "Well, Harry,
are you prepared for your bridal supper?"

She hesitated, hanging back a little. "I don't feel
like a viscountess, Richard."

"Nonsense." He patted his pocket, smiling down
at her. "Lady Sherborne, you have the marriage
lines to prove it. And if you'd change your dress
before your food grows cold, you'd best hurry."

Inside, she followed the innkeeper's wife up the
stairs to the chamber given them. It was, while not
large, neatly furnished and clean, and fine porcelain
lamps lit the room, giving it a cozy appearance. One

of the servants brought up her worn and cracked leather portmanteau, setting it on a bench inside the door. And Richard's driver carried in his traveling bag and a spare pair of boots.

After they left, she removed her gown and drew out her best dress, discovering it to be sadly creased, much more so than the travel-wrinkled one she'd worn. Taking the back of her hairbrush, she tried to smooth out the worst of it, but it really required the services of a good dresser or lady's maid.

"Harry . . . ?"

Richard stepped in and stopped, his eyes drawn to the swell of her breasts against the thin, soft cotton camisole that stretched over her zona. For a moment his mouth went dry as unexpected desire flooded through him. She saw the change in his expression and instinctively backed away, her hands clutching her creased dress. He recognized her fear and, trying to keep his voice normal, moved closer.

"Do you need help with your gown, my dear? You'd best finish dressing that we may eat."

There was only the wall behind her now, and he was so near she could feel the heat of his body. She brought the dress up higher.

"Afraid, Harry?" he asked softly. "You've no need to be, you know. 'Tis Richard—we have known each other for years, haven't we?"

Telling himself that he had to go slowly with her and not rush his fences, he took the dress from her nerveless fingers and lifted it up, holding it over her head. It was, he reflected with a trace of irony, the first time he'd ever sought to seduce by dressing a woman. To her amazement, he slipped the gown onto her neck and pulled it down about her shoulders, straightening it over her back and hips, smoothing the slim skirt downward. She sucked in her breath and stood very still as his hands moved over her body. His touch was light, but it was as though his fingers were fire.

He could see her swallow, see the faint, purplish blood vessels pulse in her neck, and he could feel her body tense as she closed her eyes to hide from him. Slowly he turned her around and began hooking the back of her dress, tracing the edge of her neckline with his fingertips. Strands of hair straggled from the severely twisted coil at the back of her head. Lifting them, curling them around his knuckle, he bent to brush his lips there.

She'd expected nothing like what she felt. Even his breath rushing against her skin burned her. "Please," she whispered weakly, shuddering as her skin turned to gooseflesh all over her body.

It delighted him that she was not going to be cold, that she was going to respond to his man's touch with a woman's desire. Tearing himself away while he yet had any appetite left for supper, he gently tugged the pins from her hair.

"Brush your hair and let us eat, Harry. I'd not tarry overlong at my food." Then, realizing how eager he must sound, he added, "We've a long journey on the morrow."

Grateful for the excuse to turn away, she faced the slanted mirror and began dragging the silver-handled brush through the tangled mass of hair that tumbled down her back. "I'd hoped to look more presentable on my wedding day, but I look like a farmer's maid masquerading as a lady. Look at this dress, and . . . and look at this hair!" she wailed.

"I'd rather look at the rest of you, if the truth be known," he teased wickedly. "Come on, Harry, your food grows cold. Besides, there's none to see you but me."

He was holding the door for her, waiting. She took one last tug at her hair and nodded. "I suppose 'tis foolish of me to want to be pretty," she sighed, passing underneath his arm.

"Not at all. You would not be a female if you did not." Smiling, he offered his arm. "Besides, I think you have succeeded."

She would be hard-put later to describe any dish she'd eaten, but it was all good, as far as she could remember. Indeed, she supposed it must be the wine, for everything blurred but an overwhelming awareness of the man seated across from her. As the covers were removed, he leaned back against the wall, his blue eyes intent on her, his glass raised.

"To you, Harry."

There was a warmth, an intimacy there that she'd never seen before, and it sent a thrill through her. Slowly she raised her own glass in acceptance, drinking to herself. Then, giggling self-consciously, she set it down. "I must surely be foxed, Richard."

"No, but you have had enough, I think." He reached across to take the glass, setting it down on the linen tablecloth. "Are you ready to retire?"

Sudden fear assailed her, and she panicked. What if she did not please him? What if she gave him a disgust of her ignorance? And what if she did not like what he would do to her? "Uh . . ."

"Harry, you are quaking like a schoolboy about to be birched," he chided.

"I . . . I should like to go up first, I think."

"All right."

She climbed the stairs with her thoughts tumbling wildly, torn by what she feared would happen if she displeased him, afraid and yet intrigued by the change she'd seen in him earlier. She closed the door and leaned on the bedpost weakly, gaining courage.

"I changed my mind, Harry," he whispered low, coming in behind her. "I'd rather undress you myself."

"No!"

"Harry . . ." She clutched the bedpost as if it were some sort of life raft when he lifted her thick hair off her neck. "Harry, I've no intention of being a married monk."

"Tomorrow—"

"Tonight." His hand slid down to the hooks of her dress, separating the first one. "The sooner all is natural between us, the better 'twill be." He felt her stiffen and tremble as the second one gave way. "Listen to me . . ." With one arm he turned her around to face him; with the other, he continued unhooking the dress. "I swear you that I shall do nothing you dislike."

"You cannot know that!" she cried.

"I know. Unlike you, I know what I am about."

"Please. 'Tis so sudden, and I—" Her words stopped abruptly as the last hook came loose and he slipped his hand under the released fabric, touching the bare skin of her back, kneading the tense muscles of her shoulder. "Richard, I—"

"Shhhh. Trust me, Harry."

He leaned closer now, brushing his lips against her ear as his hand loosened her gown and bared her shoulder. He was warm, he was vital, and he was far too near to allow her to think rationally.

"Richard . . ." she tried desperately. And then his mouth silenced hers, blotting out fear and reason. And everything that had gone before was as child's play, she thought as she gave herself up to that kiss.

Her arms slid around his waist, holding him, while his mouth took possession of hers. She was in the embrace of the man she'd loved for so long, and that was all that mattered now.

He'd expected her to be skittish and missish, but she clung to him, molding her body to his, letting him move his hands over her. It was not until he'd worked her dress, camisole, and zona down, freeing her breasts, that she resisted at all.

"No!" he croaked hoarsely as her hands came up to press against him. "Let me touch you."

She tumbled backward and fell against the bed, lying half on and half off, her dark eyes huge in her face, until he lifted her feet, swung them onto the coverlet, and followed her down. Lying above her, his body propped on one elbow, he moved more leisurely now, taking advantage of the access to her breasts. And as he massaged, gently at first, she was shocked by the sensations that washed over her. She felt the thick waves of his dark hair where it lay against her chest, and then his mouth teased first one breast and then the other, and all the while his hands were everywhere, plying and stroking until she no longer cared what he did so long as he did not stop. She felt taut as a bowstring, every fiber of her being tuned to the mesmerizing touch of his hands and the tantalizing feel of his mouth at her breast. Her hands caressed the unruly dark head ceaselessly. His free arm brushed lightly over the smooth curve of her hip as his fingers dipped lower. She went rigid with shock at first, and then, as heat spread through her whole body, she moaned low.

Abruptly he rolled back, leaving her wanting, while he undressed himself. And then he finished removing her gown and petticoat. This time, when he eased his body back over hers, it was flesh to flesh. Her arms encircled his neck, her mouth sought his eagerly, and her body gave itself up to his.

It was a union that far exceeded both their expectations as each was lost in the other, carried on the rhythmic waves of passion. Afterward he lay spent and breathless for a time, one hand tracing the rise and fall of her ribs as she sought to master her own gasping breath.

And as rational thought returned, she was suddenly afraid that he was disgusted by her wantonness. But his hand came up to brush over her bruised lips.

"Harry . . ." he managed, still panting. "Lud, girl, I don't know what came over you, but I hope 'twill always be like this between us."

"I have loved you forever," she answered simply, her own heart too full to say anything more.

12 Tired?" he asked gently.

"I own I am," she sighed.

She'd grown quieter and quieter the closer they drew to Rowe's Hill, until he'd thought she slept for a time. Her eyes had been closed, her body turned toward the window, her head resting against the crimson velvet squabs, and she'd not spoken a word for several miles. He studied her profile, the curve of her cheek, the gently waving strands of hair that persisted in straying over her temple, softening the severity of the way she wore her hair. No, she was not a beauty, but she was taking in her own way. Even now he could remember how those dark eyes of hers grew even darker with passion, and he had to admit she'd surprised him.

He'd meant to set a far faster pace, but somehow the desire to race Two Harry again paled against the pleasure his wife gave him. And for once he was glad that Hannah had not bothered to instruct her stepdaughter in the matter of the marriage bed, for she'd not imparted to Harriet that delicate revulsion so many of their class had for physical intimacy. Even now, as his eyes strayed lower to dwell on the soft curve of his wife's breasts beneath her fitted pelisse, he counted himself fortunate. If he'd had to marry years before he planned, if he'd had to wed anyone, it was just as well that it had

been Harry, for she was not likely to interfere un-
duly with his life.

He surveyed her more critically now, returning
his attention to her face. No, it was not unpleasing.
In fact, with a little artifice and the help of a good
maid, she could be made more than presentable. As
for her hair, he wondered again how it would look
cropped and curled in the current fashion, covered
in a stylish bonnet that just framed her face. Would
it wave riotously as it had done when she was but
a little girl, or had she outgrown that? No, she was
not unpleasing at all, he decided as he revised his
earlier opinion that she would never have taken.
Her shyness gone, she was far more appealing even
than he'd remembered from those long years ago.

No, she was not unpleasing at all, he told himself
yet again, and then wondered with a start if perhaps
he could not come to love her. He could do far
worse, and he knew it. Only last winter had his
friend Halbertson wed his Incomparable, and
already he'd confided that he'd set up a very pretty
bit of fluff in a snug house in Harley Street. As for
the Incomparable, he'd added bitterly, she was
naught but a cold, selfish shrew. Well, of all that
could be said of Harry, she was certainly not given
to freaks of distemper, nor did he think she'd be
inclined to spend his blunt excessively. Years of
enduring Hannah's parsimony had made comfort
an extravagance in her eyes. Indeed, she'd protested
when he insisted on purchasing a pretty shawl in
one of the towns they'd passed through.

As if she were aware of his scrutiny now, she
twisted in the seat and shifted the weight of her
small, slight frame to the other side. And as a
particularly rebellious lock strayed across her face,
she brushed it away.

"You are very quiet, my dear."

"Yes."

"Is aught amiss?"

"No." She sighed heavily again before meeting his eyes. "I hate going back, I suppose."

"If 'tis Hannah you fear, you have no reason now, my dear. Indeed, you need not be above what is civil until your things are packed." He leaned across the seat, placing his hands on her shoulders. "But if it worries you, leave Hannah to me."

"She'll be very vexed with me."

"Harry, 'tis of no matter what she thinks anymore. You are my wife, Lady Sherborne, now. There's naught else she can do to you." Releasing her, he sat back.

"I suppose you are right."

'I know I am right." He looked out the window at the lowering sun and then pulled his watch from his coat pocket, flipping open the case. " 'Tis nearly six and will be dark soon."

"We could stay at the Cock and Crown in the village," she ventured hopefully.

"No, for I sent word ahead to Rowe's Hill. I expect they will hold supper for us."

She fell silent again, lost in thoughts of her own. The past week since her marriage had been the best time in her life, and she was loath to return to a world where she would have to share her husband with others. It was so wonderful to mean something to another person, to be listened to, to be liked if not loved. And the fact that Richard had chosen to miss running Two Harry in the first races at Doncaster must surely mean that he was enjoying her company nearly as much as she was enjoying his.

And what company it was. She blushed to think of how it had been ever since that first night. They'd stopped early each evening, partaken of elegant private suppers in excellent inns, and retired to continue the discovery and exploration of each other. And she reveled in the closeness of being loved by him—in his kindness, his companionship, his extraordinary handsomeness: in everything about him. To her it seemed he lavished his attention on her, giving her that which she'd lacked for so long.

"Well, Harry, you'd best buck up," she heard him say. "By the looks of it, we have reached the lane to Rowe's Hill."

The familiar line of oak trees, fully leaved now from the milder temperatures and the spring rains, stood sentinel like soldiers the length of the long, rutted drive. A wave of loneliness washed over Harriet almost by habit as she stared at the large stone house at the end. Home, she thought bitterly, was naught but the place of fourteen years' misery.

Richard watched the parade of ever-more-sobering emotions cross her face. "Harry," he said softly, sliding across the seat to take her into his arms, " 'tis but for one night. Then I care not if we ever see either of them again."

Her hand sought his, clasping it tightly. "You cannot know how very glad I am to have you," she whispered as the carriage rolled to a halt.

"Lud, what a fond, foolish pair we are become," he murmured back, bending to drop a light kiss on her soft hair.

Her papa and stepmama were there to greet them, Sir John beaming as though he'd discovered he owned the East India Company, Hannah staring almost through her. And while Richard turned back to direct which bags should be left in the carriage boot, her father patted her heartily. Hannah, on the other hand, leaned forward and hissed under her breath, "Lady Sherborne indeed! You scheming minx!"

Harriet drew back, feeling for all the world like a chastened child, and then she reminded herself that whether Hannah liked it or not, she *was* Richard's wife. "And we are both well-served, Mama, for we shall be rid of each other," she retorted low.

"Here, now, Hannah!" her father boomed, unaware of the undercurrent between his wife and daughter. "Are we not proud? Our Harriet a viscountess! Lady Sherborne! What a sly puss— wouldn't take Thornton for she had her cap set on Sherborne here all along!"

"It was no such thing," Harriet protested faintly, blushing as Richard turned back to her.

"No, no—mustn't think we are not pleased, missy, for we are! Sherborne! And a devilish handsome fellow in the bargain!"

Embarrassed that Richard should hear her father carry on so, Harriet mumbled something nearly incoherent, hoping that her father would cease before he'd made a complete fool of himself. It was one thing to wish to get rid of a daughter hopelessly on the shelf, quite another to chortle so loudly. But despite her desperate glances, Sir John clapped Richard on the shoulder, drawing him away from her.

"And you, sirrah, have business with me in the morning, I think. There is, after all, the matter of settlements. And do not be telling me what you cannot afford, for having been trustee, I know every penny you are worth."

"Papa!"

" 'Tis all right, Harry," Richard assured her. "Despite whatever it is you fear, I do not fleece easily."

"Fleece? *Fleece*, sirrah? What manner of speech is that when you are referring to your papa-in-law?" Sir John grumbled. "I should be an unnatural parent were I not concerned for my daughter's well-being!"

"Papa!" she wailed desperately, fearful that her father's greed would somehow spoil her newfound happiness.

"I said 'tis all right," Richard repeated, taking her hand and holding it. To her father he nodded. "I shall be happy to discuss the matter of Harry's welfare in the morning, sir, but just now she is tired and in need of supper."

"Supper? Yes, yes, of course—so are we all. Hannah, when does Cook mean to serve, d'ye think?"

"Supper awaits," his wife answered grimly.

"Then there's but time to freshen, is there? Go make yourselves presentable before 'tis not fit to eat," Sir John urged. Then, turning back toward his study, he started chuckling again. "A viscountess! Who'd ever have thought the chit could do it, I ask you?" he inquired of himself.

Richard rose early, taking care not to disturb Harriet, who slept as though exhausted. It was as well to let her sleep and miss her father's ire, for he meant to tell his uncle that he had not the least intention of settling so much as a farthing on her unnatural parents. No, it was to be fifteen thousand on Harriet herself, with another five thousand pounds set aside for her on the birth of his heir. Beyond that, he'd see she had a decent allowance to keep her afloat from quarter day to quarter day. And he still meant to split Two Harry's winnings evenly.

He dressed quickly, without the services of a

valet, and walked back to the bed to look down on his sleeping wife. She lay on her side, her dark hair spilling over her pillow and tangling in wild disarray, while her arm cradled her head and her knees were draw up almost to her stomach. She looked far younger than her twenty-four years, childlike and vulnerable. But there had been nothing childish about her the night before. He reached down, pulled the covers up over her shoulder, and tiptoed from the room.

"About early, my lord?" Thomas asked him.

"So it would seem. Is anyone else down?"

"Sir John has already breakfasted, and I've not seen Lady Rowe yet. But I am to tell you that Cook has food ready whenever you wish it."

"'Now would be fine."

The young footman hesitated, and then he blurted out, "Beggin' your lordship's pardon for saying it, but 'tis glad we all are that you took Miss Harriet."

"Thank you, Thomas."

"Them as is here never cared for her as they ought, sir."

"I know, but that time is over now. You need not worry for Lady Sherborne."

Richard breakfasted alone, seated at one end of the long mahogany table, while the footman paraded back and forth with porridge, sausages, coddled eggs, and muffins. Finally, as the last covers were removed and strong coffee served, Thomas confided further, " 'Twould be a pleasure to serve you, my lord—indeed, if you should ever have need of a lower footman, I should like to apply."

"That would be Miss Harriet's—Lady Sherborne's—decision, but you may apply to her."

"Thank you, my lord."

Even as he emerged from the empty dining room,

Richard could hear voices coming from Sir John's
study. Squaring his shoulders against the unpleasantness he was certain to encounter, he
decided there was no time like the present to
dispose of the matter of settlements. It was not as
though he owed Sir John anything for the twenty-
four years of neglect he'd visited on his daughter,
after all.

He had his hand almost to the door, ready to
knock, when he heard his aunt say, "I did not think
the girl had the wits to do it, but I'd have to say she
played her part well."

"Harriet is not the slow-top you would have her,
my dear," his uncle's voice carried through the
paneled door. "Forty thousand the boy's got,
Hannah—forty thousand! I'd begun to think she
could not do it, thought we'd have to take Thornton
instead, but I'll give my Harriet credit when all's
done—the gel did it right this time!"

"As sly as Siddons, running away like that. You
were right—'twas that that did the trick I'll
warrant."

"Oh, she knew what she was about—forty
thousand pounds, my dear! I tell you, when they
ain't got looks, they've got to have guile."

"Well, she has a surfeit of that, all right," Hannah
sniffed. "Though I own I did not wish to see a
member of my own family trapped like that."

"Aye, like a hare in a trap, she got him!" Sir John
chortled. "And I'll not settle for less than if she were
a duke's daughter! Did you see the way he looked
at her last night? Got him eating like a cat at cream,
I'll be bound!"

"You forget 'tis my own nephew you and Harriet
think to fleece," Hannah protested. "I cannot wish
to see him be overgenerous to her."

Stunned, Richard dropped his hand, drawing

away. A cold, sick feeling knotted his stomach. He'd been duped, deceived, taken in by his step-cousin's wiles. It did not seem possible, but it was so. He'd just heard it of her parents, spoken when they did not mean to be overheard. It had been a plot to trap him, to ensnare his wealth before he had even had a chance to spend it himself. The awful thought stole over him that she'd known Mrs. Thornton would not be at home, that Sir John must've been laughing up his sleeve all the while he was berating and cornering him, insisting that she'd been compromised. No, Edwin Thornton had never been the target; they'd set their collective hat on far bigger game.

The sick feeling in the pit of his stomach dissipated slowly, replaced by cold anger. They'd made a fool of him. Among the three of them, they'd plotted for his gold. Well, he'd have none of it.

"Is aught amiss?" Thomas asked behind him.

"Huh? Oh, not any longer," he snapped. Then, recovering himself under the footman's puzzled stare, he ordered, "I shall require paper, ink, and a pen, if you please."

It was past noon when Harriet finally came down, grateful that her husband had let her sleep through any unpleasantness. There was no sign of anyone in the lower hall except Thomas, who lingered nervously, Richard's letter tucked in his jacket.

"Miss Har . . . Lady Sherborne, that is," he whispered low, motioning her over to the doorway that led to the kitchen.

"Thomas, have you seen my husband?" she asked, suddenly anxious at the thought she might have to face Hannah alone ere they left.

"Aye." He drew out the sealed envelope. "He left you this."

"Left?" The blood drained from her face as a terrible premonition stole over her, telling her something was very wrong. "He left?"

"About two hours ago, and Sir John and Lady Rowe are in a taking over it."

"I see." There must've been a terrible quarrel, then, but why had he not waited for her? He must be coming back—he'd but gone to the Marches' for Two Harry. Yes, that was it, she told herself firmly. He'd gone after the horse, then would come back for her and they would leave. But what could her father have done to make him so angry that he would not tell her of it first? With shaking fingers she pulled out the letter and began to read the strong, bold script inside with disbelief. And part of her died.

"Harriet," it began. Not "Dearest Harry," nor "Harry," even—just "Harriet." With sinking heart she read on.

Having discovered your deceit, I have decided to remove myself from this house without further discourse between us. There is naught that you could say that would compensate for the betrayal I have felt today.

By the time you receive this, I shall be on my way to follow the racing circuit with Two Harry, something I should have done from the beginning. Perhaps when the season is over, I may be able to face you without anger and bitterness.

I will continue to send your share of the purses to London, and should you need more, you may draw upon my accounts there in an amount not exceeding five hundred pounds per quarter. You need only present your marriage lines to my solicitor, Mr. Robert Campbell, in his office in

Lombard Street near St. Michael's Alley, I am sure.

Upon my return, we shall discuss what shall be done concerning this unfortunate marriage.

Sherborne

Sherborne. She'd not called him by his title in her life. She crushed the paper in her hand and stared about her in blank dismay. He was not coming back, she told herself bleakly, trying to assimilate the whole, but all she could really understand was that he'd left her. He'd left her alone to face Hannah's scorn. The ache in her chest was unbearable, and yet she had to think. What? What had she done? Why had he left? And what on earth could she do? She had no answers to any of it. Her briefly happy world in ruins around her, she leaned her head against the wall and cried.

"Miss . . . milady," Thomas tried helplessly, "if there is aught I—"

"Oh, Thomas! My . . . my h-husband h-has left me, and . . . and I am the most m-miserable of females!" she choked out, unable to control the sobs that shook her shoulders and racked her body.

Shocked, he could think of nothing to say, but he finally mumbled, "Mayhap 'twas but a row."

"B-but we never q-quarreled!"

"You'll come about, m-milady. Here, now— naught's to be gained by cryin' your eyes out, is there?" He looked about to make sure none saw, and then he reached a comforting hand to her shoulder. "Miss Harriet, there's all of us here as cares about you, and—"

"Oh, Thomas," she whispered, turning her tear-streaked face into his shoulder, "I cannot bear it!"

"Harriet! Harriet!"

"Here, miss, you cannot let her see you so," the footman whispered, stepping back hastily. Proferring a wilted handkerchief, he added significantly, "She'll have a rare time if you let her, now, won't she?"

Nodding, she blew her nose noisily and tried to compose herself. Whatever had happened between her and Richard, she could not let Hannah know of it, else she'd never live it down. Wiping her wet face hastily, she thrust the cloth into her pocket just as her stepmama came into the hall.

"There you are, you ungrateful girl! 'Tis hours and more we have waited for Sherborne to discuss matters at hand, and 'twould seem he has disappeared! Your papa is less than pleased, missy!"

In less distressful times, Harriet would have been cowed by the tone in the older woman's voice, but now she was beyond caring. She sucked in her breath, let it out slowly, and faced Hannah. "I am Harriet Standen, Lady Sherborne, Mama, and 'missy' no more," she managed evenly, despite the thudding of her heart. "And as for Sherborne, he has been called away." She lifted up the crumpled paper in her hand, letting her stepmama see only that he'd written. "He begs your pardon, but 'twas unavoidable."

Hannah's eyes bore into her, but for once Harriet held her ground, refusing to blench beneath that cold stare. "And I am to ask Papa for the loan of his carriage, that I may proceed to Richlands and await my husband there." Her chin came up as she mustered what dignity she could. "The matter of settlements will, of course, have to wait until the racing season is over."

Hannah was speechless.

"Here, missy, what nonsense is this?" her father

thundered from the doorway of his study. "Sherborne gone, you say?"

"Yes, and I will be leaving also, Papa. No doubt Ri . . . Sherborne will write a letter of explanation to you later. Now, if you will but excuse me, I must prepare for my journey to Richlands. And I shall require the traveling coach."

"You . . . you cannot ride that far alone, girl!" Sir John expostulated. " 'Tisn't done!"

Harriet looked past Hannah to the footman. "I shan't be alone, Papa—I have just engaged Thomas."

To his credit, the young man did not betray his surprise when both Sir John and Lady Rowe turned to stare at him. Flicking a small numb of lint from his jacket front, he managed to murmur, "Just so, sir. I spoke to Lord Sherborne of it but this morning."

"But you have no maid! And I'll not let you take—"

"Er . . . I believe 'twas Lord Sherborne's express wish to engage m'sister Millie," Thomas added.

"I did not know you had a sister employed as a maid!" Hannah retorted angrily. "As for you, missy, how is it that Sherborne did not think to apprise me of this turn, I ask you?" she demanded.

"I told you—'twas unexpected."

Hannah peered even more closely at her now. "You have been weeping!" she accused triumphantly.

"I did not wish him to go."

"Humph! Sounds havey-cavey business to me!"

"Papa, I shall write when I reach Richlands," Harriet promised, eager to escape. "If you will but order the carriage, I really must follow my husband's express wishes, do you not think?"

"Well, as to that . . ." He hesitated, rubbing his chin as he often did when faced with a struggle between his wife and his daughter. "Damme, Hannah! She ain't mine to tell anything anymore! She's Sherborne's! And if he's wanting her to follow him today, stands to reason she ought to do it! There! I have said it! Run along, missy, and get what you require."

"John—"

"My mind is set, Hannah! A woman must do as her husband says!" he snapped, brushing his wife's protests aside. "The carriage will be ready within the hour! Though I think it remiss of the boy to neglect the settlements," he muttered under his breath. "But that ain't to say as he won't be back."

His piece said, he stalked back to the refuge of his study with his wife on his heels. Harriet raised her eyes gratefully to the footman who'd supported her. "You do not have to go, you know. As it is, I have no notion of my welcome."

"I'll come. 'Tis sick I am of her overbearing ways myself."

"*Do* you have a sister, Thomas?" she inquired hopefully, thinking somehow that her arrival would be less remarked if she had a maid to support her.

"Aye. She ain't a maid precisely, but I daresay she can learn."

13 Standing in the immense entry hall at Richlands, waiting whilst the butler sought out the housekeeper for her, Harriet experienced very real qualms about having come to Richard Standen's primary country estate. It was far grander than anything of her imagination, and everything from the starchy butler to the cavernous marble-floored hall, the broad sweeping staircase, the high gold-trimmed ceiling, and the immense hundred-lamp chandelier gave her a very real sense of inferiority. Even the dozen or so Standen ancestors stared balefully down from portraits that lined the entrance hall, each seeming to tell her she had no right to be there.

To calm her very real fears, she moved from one to the other of the ornately framed pictures, studying each one. Hannah had boasted once that the Standens were an ancient and noble family, but Harriet had not realized until then just how old they were. One portrait in particular caught her attention, and she stepped closer to read the engraved brass beneath. *Robert Standen, Baron Lynford, 1545-1589.* She cocked her head and looked upward, trying to discover any resemblance between the fellow in the Elizabethan collar and the present Viscount Sherborne. But 'twas too distant, she decided, moving on to the last one. *Henry*

Standen, Fifth Viscount Sherborne, 1765-1802.
Richard's father, another Harry, who'd died the
year her father had married Hannah Belford,
Richard's aunt on his mother's side. Well, he looked
much like his son, she decided, in his painted eyes.
Her gaze traveled slowly to the tall, elegant woman
on the wall beside him. *Catherine Belford Standen,
1771-1799.* She'd been but twenty or twenty-one
when her son was born, and only twenty-eight when
she'd died. What had Richard said of them—that
they'd had no children other than him because they
did not deal well together? The lovely dark-haired
woman wore an infathomable expression, as though
she carried her thoughts with her to her grave.
These then were Richard's parents.

A stab of pain cut through her as she looked at
them, and she felt betrayed all over again. Was it
like this between men and women—did the women
love and the men hurt them always?

"I am Mrs. Creighton, Lord Sherborne's housekeeper. I believe Mr. Stubbs said you wished to
speak with me."

For a moment Harriet's mouth seemed almost too
dry for speech as she spun to face a middle-aged
woman dressed almost as well as she. But as
Thomas already had her portmanteau through the
door, she knew some explanation must be in order.
Behind her, the girl Millie stared upward in awe at
the huge chandelier, like a veritable gapeseed come
to town.

"So nice to meet you, Mrs. Creighton." She forced
herself to smile at the older woman. "Did my
husband not tell you to expect me? Dear me, but
how dreadfully shameful of him." She held out her
hand. "I am Lady Sherborne."

"There must be some mistake," the housekeeper
answered after a lengthy silence. "Lord Sherborne

is not at home. He went to race his horse at Newmarket."

"Of course he did." Harriet's heart thudded as Mrs. Creighton looked at her with utter disbelief. "And Two Harry won. Oh, dear, did he not tell you of me at all? I am—was—Harriet Rowe, and we were wed in Bath last week."

"No, he did not."

"And this is Thomas, my footman, and Millie, my maid."

The look the housekeeper gave the girl, who still gawked shamelessly about her, was plainly skeptical. "Rowe?" she murmured finally, turning her attention again to Harriet. "Relations of his then."

"Yes. His mama and my stepmama were sisters." Harriet tried another smile. "But for now, I am quite fatigued from my journey from Rowe's Hill and I should like to freshen before I dine. I pray you will show me to my chamber. And I shall require lodging for Thomas and Millie."

There was another pregnant pause as the housekeeper hesitated, and Harriet determined to show authority. "Mrs. Creighton, I do not like to repeat myself."

"He did not say to expect anyone . . ." Then, after a slight hesitation she added, ". . . my lady."

"Then I suggest you send to his lordship, apprising him of your concern. In the meantime, I shall still require my chamber, thank you. Come, Millie," she ordered grandly. "We shall follow Mrs. Creighton, who seems to be under the misapprehension that I do not belong in my own house." And when the housekeeper did not budge, she sighed and opened her reticule. "I consider this insolence of the highest order, and so I shall tell my husband, but since you appear to doubt me, I will for this once show you my marriage lines. I do not, however, expect to find this necessary again."

The woman stood silently as Harriet unfolded the document for her, and there she saw the unmistakably bold signature. "Your pardon, my lady," she managed, betraying her shock. "Why he would allow such a thing, I cannot think . . . that is, but *of course* you must be welcomed to Richlands. Mr. Stubbs," she addressed the butler who now hovered curiously behind Harriet, "you will have someone carry up Lady Sherborne's case to the master's chamber." And to Harriet she unbent enough to confide, "There's been none in her ladyship's rooms since she left them, so I expect he will want you in his. I mean, naught else's fit for your ladyship, I shouldn't think."

It was Harriet's first small victory over Richard's household. "Thank you, Mrs. Creighton. Once I am unpacked and changed, I should like to look at the last Lady Sherborne's chamber, for I mean to have it refitted to my taste. Oh, and I should also like the direction of a competent seamstress."

"As to that, there is a very good woman in Lower Weston, my lady. Perhaps Stubbs could send one of the grooms over with a request that she attend you here tomorrow."

Attend her at Richlands? Harriet could barely conceive of such a thing, but then, she'd not been a viscountess before, she reminded herself as she followed Mrs. Creighton up the grand staircase. The soles of her kid slippers seemed to sink in the thick carpet runners that covered the treads.

"When do you expect his lordship to return?" the housekeeper asked her.

"As to that, I am not certain. I believe he means to race Two Harry at all the major tracks while he can. The season is so short, after all."

"Surely he does not mean to stay away until fall."

"As long as Two Harry wins, I would not begin to guess when he will come home," Harriet answered dryly

The older woman stopped in front of a pair of double doors at the end of the hallway. "This is Lord Sherborne's chamber, my lady. Hers is beside it. 'Tis the one we have just passed."

The door swung open, revealing a chamber of stately elegance. Harriet, used to the small room at Rowe's Hill, could scarce credit her eyes, for it looked to her as though Richard Standen lived in sinful, regal splendor. As her eyes traveled from the ornate chandelier to the moiré taffeta walls to the heavy Aubusson rug to the twin marble fireplaces at either end of the huge room, she was overwhelmed.

"His lordship does not particularly like it, or so Mr. O'Neal would have us believe—says 'tis over-large and pretentious, I am told. Mr. O'Neal," she added with a hint of disapproval, "is Irish and full of gossip."

"Mr. O'Neal . . ." Harriet murmured faintly, still looking at the room.

"Oh, mum!" Millie breathed. "Ain't it grand!"

"Mr. O'Neal is his lordship's valet, but he is on holiday just now, as Lord Sherborne did not think he would need him at Newmarket. Lord Sherborne," Mrs. Creighton stated flatly, "did not expect to be gone long, or so Mr. O'Neal was told."

"Yes, well, I daresay his plans have changed."

" 'Tis to be expected of a man and his sport, I suppose." Mrs. Creighton drew open the heavy damask draperies, admitting the late-afternoon sun. "Would your ladyship be wishful of anything else? Or will your maid tend to everything?" Once again she glanced at Millie and shuddered. "While we have no lady's maids here, madam, there is one who appears to have some skill with hair."

"No, no. Everything is fine."

"We dine at seven—country hours, you know."

With that, she was gone, leaving Harriet to stare in dismay at her new surroundings. She'd known from childhood that Richard was rich, but she'd never guessed it was anything like this. Her small loan of one thousand pounds must have seemed terribly insignificant. No, she reminded herself fiercely, it was not. It mattered not what he possessed—the fact remained that at the particular time he'd needed her money desperately. It was that fact that made it possible to do what she did now. He was in her debt.

As she looked around her, she could not conceive that her father could have ever been to Richlands. Or that he had managed to keep his hands out of Richard's pockets when her step-cousin was a boy. But then she supposed it must have been the influence of Richard's maternal uncle, who'd been co-trustee until his death the year before. But Hannah must have known. Not that she ever mentioned her sister Catherine even in passing. It gave Harriet a certain satisfaction to think that perhaps the lovely Lady Sherborne had quite cast her elder sister in the shade. Only jealousy could have accounted for Hannah's lack of interest in Richlands. What she could not possess, she refused to care about.

"Oh, mum—over here!" Millie breathed. "There's a dressing room! Did you ever see the like of it?"

But Harriet was no longer attending anything. She'd opened a drawer in a large carved mahogany chest, discovering the neatly folded piles of Richard's shirts. Stricken, she closed the drawer and her eyes at the same time. The now familiar pain of betrayal cut through her and left a dull ache in her breast. Why? Why had he let her love him? And why, oh why, had he left?

"I say, mum . . . Oh, my, are you all right?"

"No." Her face crumpled piteously as she turned away.

The girl's arms went around her, hugging her close. "Here, now—don't you cry none, mum. Thomas told me how it was with you."

Harriet fought the urge to have a really good cry, and won. Slowly mastering herself, she smiled tremulously. "No. My own mama was used to say when I was a little girl that spilt milk never wipes itself up."

"Eh?"

"I think she meant we must take it upon ourselves to help ourselves—or some such thing."

"I dunno. I only heard about cryin' over it myself. But if it lightens your spirit, you think what you want it to mean," the girl decided, shaking her head.

"Just because he does not want me does not mean he shall cast me aside," Harriet added stoutly, stiffening her resolve to remain at Richlands until Richard should come home and explain himself. She, she recalled firmly, was the injured party. And she was Lady Sherborne, after all.

"Aye, you have the right of that," the girl agreed.

Thus fortified, Harriet turned her attention to what she would do. For the next few weeks at least she would be mistress of a great house. She would use her freedom to improve herself, to forget Hannah and her hateful tongue. Resolutely she sat down at Richard's desk and drew out the ink jar, pen, and paper. The first thing she would do was direct his solicitor to release her first quarter's allowance. The second would be to obtain her remaining thousand pounds. And then she would refurbish the other chamber as befitted her new station in life. In short, she would learn to face life's disappointments from a position of strength. And if Richard Standen did not like what she did, he would just have to evict her. But whatever happened, she *would* have an explanation of him. He could not destroy her pride and humiliate her and not answer for it.

As the pen stroked across the paper, she was startled by the feel of something soft and warm rubbing across the top of her foot. Looking down, she saw a ball of multicolored fur curling playfully around her ankle. And then a pair of decidedly round, decidedly unmatched eyes winked at her.

"Heloise!"

Reminding herself that the cat could not possibly remember her, she bent to lift her up. "So you have become used to Richard's bed, have you? Disgraceful!" But she nuzzled the small dark nose as she said it. For answer, Heloise pawed at the loose tendrils of hair that framed her face.

"There's a cat in Lord Sherborne's chamber?" Millie asked in surprise. "I did not think lords had such creatures in the house."

"Actually, he has three of them," Harriet murmured, holding the calico close and listening to her loud purr. "Oh, Helly, I have missed you."

"Well, my da wouldn't have 'em anywheres but the barn, and we didn't live like this. But there's no unnerstandin' the Quality."

Harriet felt the pink tongue rasping against her neck like the back of a file. And, as low as her spirits were, she knew she had something to love again. "You know," she whispered against the soft fur, "as soon as I am finished with my letters, I mean to discover your mama and your brother also."

14 For nearly two months Harriet was able to immerse herself in self-improvement. She not only learned the names of virtually every person employed in the running of the house, the stables, the barns, and the immense park, but also asked questions of them until she was reasonably certain of what each one did. Moreover, at the end of each day she retired to Richard's chamber and made endless lists to ensure that she did not forget any of it. It was, she reasoned, the only way to learn how to manage her new home.

And the more questions she asked, the more Richard's staff, flattered by her interest, unbent to answer. She soon discovered that beneath Mrs. Creighton's rather stern exterior lay a competent, basically pleasant person. Stubbs was perhaps the more difficult task, but after having lived with Hannah for fourteen years, Harriet found him not impossible. Her willingness to view everyone in the house as a valuable person, coupled with a little genuine praise and a little flattery, soon had almost every servant from the housekeeper and the butler to the lowest footman and tweeny agreeing "the young mistress will do very well."

As for the matter of where she would stay when Richard came home, she set about almost instantly to refurbish the last viscountess's rooms, choosing not the ornate, opulent golds and reds she discovered there, but rather simple roses and greens. The plaster rosettes and intricate ceiling moldings had to be tolerated, because as much as she could change the smaller things, she did not think she dared alter the structural character of the suite.

One thing she did discover quickly: tradesmen—from the greengrocer, the carpenters, the painters, to the local modiste—were willing, eager even, to secure her patronage. She could have run up bills far in excess of her mother's portion and her quarter's allowance with no trouble at all had she been so inclined. And she was tempted, but as hurt and angered as she was by Richard's desertion, she still could not bring herself to behave so shabbily. No, she would pay as she played, she decided, giving herself a certain distinction amongst the neighborhood.

The local seamstress, or modiste as she styled herself, came often in the first weeks of Harriet's residence at Richlands, and the result, while not earth-shaking, was quite gratifying. But perhaps it was Harriet's desire to prove Richard wrong, or perhaps she merely hoped that a stunning wardrobe would somehow compensate for what she perceived to be her plainness, for after having acquired enough day dresses and walking dresses to see her through a few days in London, she determined to visit a truly fashionable modiste.

Thus, armed with several copies of *La Belle Assemblée*, favorite pages turned back at the corners, she embarked for the city with Millie and Alice, another maid impressed from belowstairs for her ability to do hair. Rather than invading Richard's town house and facing the task of subduing the servants there all over again, she took up four days' residence in a moderately fashionable hotel. At Madame Cecile's, plates were selected, fabrics were chosen, and gowns were ordered. Even the seemingly interminable fittings did not bother her save for a slight soreness of her breasts.

She was truly enjoying her freedom, thinking that the life of a married woman, particularly one whose husband was out of town, was not bad by half. She'd even resumed riding. And her determined pursuit of self-improvement provided a much-needed distraction from the pain of her husband's desertion. In short, she was now more furious than anything else. But in the back of her mind she had to admit that she hoped he would be pleasantly shocked when he saw her, that he would realize just what he had so callously abandoned. For she meant to see him squirm.

It was on the trip back from London that she became truly sick. Not merely ill—sick. At first she thought she was but a trifle travel queasy, and then she decided it was the June heat, but by the time she'd shot the cat, as her brother would have said, some five times in the space of as many hours, she began to worry. And when she did not get better once she was back at Richlands, she consented to see the local physician.

"You are, I am quite positive, increasing, Lady Sherborne," he told her.

"What? But I have just bought new clothes!" she wailed, unwilling to accept that such a thing could happen.

"Alas, but I cannot help that," he murmured, surprised by her reaction. "But the other will quite take care of itself. Within the space of a month or so, the nausea will pass."

She sat alone in the great library at Richlands long after he left, too stunned to think. She carried Richard Standen's child. She carried the heir to all that surrounded her. He'd married her in haste, gotten a child of her, and left her, not knowing it. At first she felt terribly cheated, as though fate had once again turned against her. She'd planned how she would look down the last touch when he came home, and now, if he ever did get there, she would be fat and increasing! And if he did once again turn to her, it would be because of the child she carried!

"My lady?" One of the downstairs maids peeked around the door. "Cook is wishful of knowing when you would have supper?"

The very thought of food sent a shudder of revulsion through her, and for a moment she thought she was going to be ill again. "I . . .I do not believe I shall dine tonight," she managed through clenched teeth.

"She said she would send up toast and tea to your bedchamber if you should prefer it."

"No."

The room grew darker, and still she sat, for once allowing herself to wonder where Richard was just then. When she'd been in London, a visit to her bank had yielded the information that she was some three thousand pounds richer than when he left, indicating that Two Harry was doing very well indeed. But there'd been absolutely no word from him. Of course, he did not exactly have her direction, she owned judiciously. But then neither did he care. What had he written in the awful letter? *Upon my return, we shall discuss what shall be done concerning this unfortunate marriage.* Well, fate had certainly dealt him a blow also, for now he could scarce divorce her, not whilst she carried his child.

"Merrrow."

There was a soft rubbing against her leg, followed by a leap into her lap. Athena turned around several times, kneading against Harriet's still reasonably flat stomach, and then she stood on her hind legs to place paws on either side of her mistress's neck, leaning forward to nuzzle nose to nose. It was much the way she used to comfort Harriet when Hannah's tongue became unbearable.

For a time Harriet held her close, stroking the long, slender cat's back, drawing comfort from her. "What a blue-deviled pair we are, Athena," she murmured. "You are unhappy because the last of your litter is gone, and I am unhappy because I am increasing."

The cat sat back on her haunches, looking at Harriet, and then she lay down, purring loudly, in her lap. And as Harriet rubbed the soft warm fur, she began to take solace from the cat. Perhaps, she mused slowly, perhaps she ought not to feel so alone. She would have the child, Richard's child—a sturdy little boy or girl—to love. Athena purred steadily now, and Harriet began to dream of her child, wondering whether it would favor her or Richard.

"You'll take sick," Mrs. Creighton chided her, coming in to light the sconces on the wall. "Your Millie's turned down your bed, Lady Sherborne, and Alice has your toast and tea ready. If you do not make it too sweet, maybe it'll set better. And if you want, I'll summon Thomas to help you up—or you may lean on me, for that matter," she added kindly.

With an effort, Harriet shifted the cat off her lap and rose. "No, I shall be fine. I am tired, 'tis all."

"Well, now, you be sure to eat, my lady. I'd not have his lordship thinking we were starving you at a time like this."

Upstairs, both Millie and Alice fussed over her, brushing her newly cropped hair and helping her into her nightrail. Alice slipped out for the tray while Millie plumped her pillows.

"You knew, did you not?"

"That you was increasing? Well, I suspected as much, what with you married in April," the girl admitted. "Just wish Lord Sherborne was here to take care of you, that's all."

"Well, he is not," Harriet snapped peevishly. Then, realizing how out-of-reason cross she must sound, she leaned back against the pillows and closed her eyes. "I'm sorry, Millie."

"I guess I ain't much of a maid, am I? Oversetting you and all like that."

"Millie—"

"No, it ain't bred in me, mum, and I know it."

"Nonsense."

"You goin' to write to him?"

"No. I have not his direction," Harriet sighed. "And I cannot see what difference 'twill make. If I've learned naught else these last months, 'tis that I can take care of myself."

"Mum?"

"What?"

"I just wanted you to know I ain't a hand t' gossip b'lowstairs any. I ain't never told 'em how it is with you."

"Thank you, Millie."

"But there's them as wants to know why he ain't here or ain't wrote."

"They are not alone," Harriet muttered dryly, wishing for Alice to return with the toast.

"Well, I told 'em you'd heard from him—last week afore we went to Lunnon. Oh, I know it ain't right to lie about such things, but letters did come from Rowe's Hill and all."

" 'Tis all right, Millie—this time. But I wish you would refrain from discussing me with anyone."

The girl hung her head. "There. I knew you was

goin' to be angered with me. But, mum, I didn't want 'em to think—"

"As 'tis none of their business, Millie, they don't need to think about it at all. But I daresay you could not help it," Harriet allowed tiredly. "Would you go see what keeps Alice? I find I shall probably be able to eat the toast, after all."

Alone again, she tried not to think of anything for a while, but the girl's words had struck home, probably because they were such a reminder of what Richard had said on their marriage. *I mean to take care of you.* Well, he had not. Bitterness welled anew inside her as she thought of how kind, how tender he'd been that night. And then he'd left her. 'Twould have been kinder not to have raised her hopes at all.

There was a faint padding across the carpet, followed by a thud on the foot of the bed. Then, with slow feline grace, Heloise made her way to the top. Almost immediately, Abelard followed, his black fur shining in contrast to the whiteness of the sheets. And on the floor, Athena paced and meowed.

"Well, you might as well join us," Harriet offered, leaning over to pick her up. "Though I warn you— there's naught coming but dry toast."

Alice returned with the tea tray, frowning at the sight of three cats on the bed. "Leave them be," Harriet ordered, reaching for the first piece of toast.

"I don't know as his lordship's going to like it when he gets home and finds three of 'em's moved into his bed. 'Twas bad enough when the funny-looking one was crawling up from the bottom, or so Mr. O'Neal said. And at least she had the decency to wait until he was asleep, instead of wantin' to eat his crumbs."

"Where is Mr. O'Neal, anyway?"

"Gone to meet his lordship somewheres in France, accordin' to Mr. Stubbs, who's heard from him. Wrote he was leavin' last week, I think."

France. Harriet's heart sank. It was as though Richard never meant to come home again. "Did Mr. O'Neal write anything else to Mr. Stubbs?" she wanted to know, despite the fact that it was highly improper to gossip with the servants.

"Only that the horse was winnin', but I guess you knew that yourself. I mean, I guess Lord Sherborne wrote you of it."

"Yes. Yes, he did."

"I just wish O'Neal'd come back," the girl added. "It don't seem right with him not fussin' about cat hair on things. He was used to complain, and Lord Sherborne'd tell him just to brush it off. But, lud, what an Irish temper O'Neal has! He'd brush and mutter, brush and mutter, until Crighton'd come up and tell him to keep his Irish cant to himself, you know. But his lordship never paid the least attention to it—just winked at me and went on." The girl grinned at Harriet. "Aye, O'Neal fussed, but the cats stayed."

"I thought Richard—Lord Sherborne—did not like cats."

"Humph! He'd put 'em out at night, and afore he'd be back to bed, that funny-looking one'd be a-hidin' under the covers. Determined little vixen, if you was to ask me. But I wasn't there, of course—I had to hear it of O'Neal in the mornings."

Harriet bit into the toast and chewed slowly, hoping fervently that when it was swallowed, it meant to stay down. "I gave him the cats, you know."

"Well, I thought they must be particular favorites, 'cause when Creighton would have put 'em outside in the barns, he wouldn't let her. Had Cook fixin' food for 'em 'cause they were homesick, he said." The maid tidied up the bedside table and hung up Harriet's dress in the wardrobe. "Ring when you are done, and I'll come back for the tray."

The toast tasted like sawdust, but Harriet forced herself to eat it. The sooner she kept something down, the sooner the awful sickness would go away, or so she hoped. She managed one slice and set the tray on the table, too tired to bother with it. Lying back once again, she closed her eyes and tried to sleep.

She was going to bear a child. Richard was in France. If he did not care for her, would he care for the child? Did he ever think of her? Would he even come back? She had no answers, but she could not help asking the questions over and over again.

15 Having completed the racing loop of Doncaster, Chester, and Derby, and not wanting to draw further attention to the fact that Two Harry was as yet unbeaten in the overnights, those races that could be entered by any thoroughbred registered the night before, Richard took Two Harry on to the Continent. There the horse could get needed experience and the oddsmakers would have less of a chance to see him before he came back and entered the more prestigious big-purse events like the 2,000 Guineas at Newmarket the following year.

During the months of June, July, August, and September, Richard ran Two Harry in everything from local fairs to sanctioned thoroughbred races in France, Germany, and Italy, losing only thrice to local favorites on difficult, unfamiliar courses. And each time Two Harry acquired too much notice, he moved on.

Even abroad, and particularly in Germany, there was considerable interest in the horse's rather unusual name, and Richard found himself having to explain its origin far more often than he cared to. It was, he began saying, merely named for two horseracing enthusiasts. But each time the matter came up, he was reminded of Harriet. In fact, despite his determined pursuit of fortune and pleasure, he thought of her far too often for his peace of mind.

Much of his racing career he owed to her—the horse's name, his racing colors, the horse itself even. More than once, after he'd won particularly lucrative or competitive races, he'd actually thought about writing to her. But each time, he'd reminded himself that she'd duped him, trapped him, taken advantage of his friendship, and wed him by deceit. But there was that about her that still nagged him, an underlying doubt. Had it not been for the fact that he'd overheard her father and Hannah laughing over it, he'd not have believed it. But it wasn't as though they knew he could hear them. And Harry had not hesitated to accept him that second time in Bath. Alone at night, in the dark silence of his bed, he puzzled over what had happened, sometimes hating her, sometimes doubting, but always wanting.

And a parade of willing widows, lovely Cyprians, and eager daughters of local nobility did little to ease the loss he felt over Harry's perfidy. And yet he was too proud to go back to her, too angered still. So he flirted, drank far too much, and wagered fortunes daily on his horse, telling himself that he'd deal with the problem of his marriage later.

By mid-September he was at a small dirt track outside Palermo, Sicily, taking bets on yet another race, when his attention was caught by a young girl in the crowd. Something about the color of her hair, the set of her chin, her almost furtive glances under her mama's watchful eye, reminded him of Harry. He stared at her, forgetting the man who haggled over odds with him, forgetting the hot sun, forgetting everything. It was as though he were looking at Harry. The girl, now aware of his fixed gaze, smiled shyly, then turned to point him out to her mother. And within the space of a few seconds he was facing her irate brother. In Sicily, he discovered, a man did not look at a female quite like that and live. It was only after he stammered out an apology, explaining that she reminded him much of his wife, that the race went on at all.

His wife. He'd said it aloud. He'd admitted he could not help thinking of her. As Two Harry crossed the finish line ahead by a length, Richard admitted defeat to himself. So she had misled him, entrapped him into marriage. Did that make her any different from the dozens of girls on the Marriage Mart, girls who flattered and flirted, spouting all manner of silliness in hopes of gaining husbands? Not really. At least Harry had had the excuse of wanting to escape Hannah. While the crowd clamored around him, while sweaty men counted out money into his hands, Richard abruptly decided to go home.

As he made arrangements for transport to England, he felt relieved. He'd go home and let her explain, and he would forgive her for her deceit. She might not be the beauty he'd once thought he wanted, but he'd take her to London, fit her out in decent gowns, and present her to the *ton* as his viscountess.

For much of the journey home he planned her entrée into society, reasoning that with him at her side she would somehow take. Having crossed the bridge between anger and acceptance, he allowed himself to think of her freely now, convincing himself that his Harry might well be an Original. By the time he docked at Dover, he was not only reconciled to the task, he actually looked forward to it. He'd punished her enough; now he would make it up to her. Besides, he could no longer deny the very physical need he felt whenever he thought of her.

Uncertain of his welcome at Rowe's Hill, he determined to travel first to Richlands, engage carpenters and painters to refurbish his mother's awful rooms, and write to Harriet from there. It would, he hoped, ease the awkwardness of his return.

At Dover he visited a jeweler and purchased a more fitting bridal gift—a diamond-and-emerald brooch. He'd hoped to discover a ring suitable to replace his, something more elegant and feminine, but decided to wait until he took her to London. A marriage ring ought to reflect the taste of the wearer, after all.

That night, after supper, he carried a bottle of the innkeeper's best Madeira upstairs and split it with Sean O'Neal, his valet. After five months of traveling town to town, inn to inn, there'd sprung up more than the relationship of lord and servant between them. The affable Irishman, Richard had discovered, was not only charming to the maids but also an excellent listener.

"What do you think, O'Neal—am I a fool or not?" he asked, leaning back and sipping reflectively from his glass.

"Well, yer honor's honor, as to that I couldn't say, but show me a man not a fool for 'em, and I'll show ye a dead one." Grinning, the valet drained his cup and refilled it. "Aye, and who's not prey to a pretty face, I ask ye—not me, anyways. But from what ye've said t' me, seems t' me the question's how high in the boughs she's goin' t' be."

"Harry?" Richard considered for a moment, then shook his head. "Harry," he pronounced definitely, "is never given to freaks of distemper."

"Beggin' yer honor's pardon, but she's a female,

ain't she? And, faith, but there's not a one of 'em as don't cut up the dust, is there, now?" O'Neal reminded him.

"No matter how angered she is, she'll be glad enough to escape her stepmama. That, at least, I have in my favor," Richard mused, finishing his wine. "And I mean to tell her I forgive her from the beginning."

"Will ye, now? Seems to me, your honor forgive me f'r sayin' it, if this Lady Rowe's all you've said o' her, 'tis yourself that'll be needin' the forgiveness."

That was one part of his conscience Richard did not want to dwell on, for more than once he'd wondered what Hannah had said after he left, only to push it aside. Whatever it was, it could not have been pleasant, he was certain. Well, this time when he took Harry from Rowe's Hill, she'd never have to go back.

Draining yet another cup of the strong wine, the valet eyed his master over the rim. "Bothers ye, don't it?"

"Yes."

"Well, I never favored one female myself, you understand, but if I was to, I think I'd f'rget the thinkin' on it and put it t' the touch. Females," he announced emphatically, "is deuced odd creatures, don't ye know? A man never knows what they'll do until they do it!"

"Just the same, I think I'll write first."

"Now, beggin' yer honor's honor, but if 'twas me . . ." The valet's grin broadened. "I'd want t' face her. Ain't one of 'em alive as don't melt f'r the blarney."

"Of which you seem to possess a surfeit. My 'honor's honor,' is it? O'Neal, if the truth were known, beneath all those groveling words, there beats the heart of a scoundrel," Richard reminded him dryly.

"Faith, but there's more'n a bit of scoundrel in all of us, I'd have to say, your honor," O'Neal agreed blithely. "But if I was goin' t' be a coward and write t' her, I'd not wait for Richlands." He held up the bottle, shaking his head. " 'Tis gone, all o' it, yer honor. Got t' get the both of us another."

Much later, after the valet had retired to sleep off the effects of too much wine, Richard sat up and tried to write. But either he was too foxed to make sense or he couldn't find the right words. Finally he crumpled the sixth sheet of paper and threw it on the floor in disgust. No, he'd have to write from Richlands, after all. And as he eased his travel-wearied body into bed, he wondered if O'Neal were right—if he were a coward not to face her.

16 The air was chilly and damp in the October afternoon, so much so that a fire blazed in the library's broad marble-faced fireplace, popping and sputtering from the wet wood Thomas had brought in. Harriet laid aside the book she'd been reading, a copy of Jane Austen's latest, ordered from London fresh off the press. But as much as she liked the story, she could scarce follow it for the drowsiness she felt. Dr. Paxton had warned her that it would be this way, that females experienced a great deal of lethargy while increasing, but she'd not been prepared for the indolence that threatened to overwhelm her. Reluctantly she drew up her knees into the chair, pulled the heavy shawl about her, and leaned her head back. Perhaps if she dozed a few minutes, it would pass . . .

She never heard the carriage roll up the drive, nor did she hear Richard order a groom to saddle Two Harry for a fast run around the training yard. The child within her shifted position and was still.

"Hallo, Stubbs. O'Neal, see to the removal of the bags, will you? I'd be repacked for the morrow." Richard stopped, his hands still on the frogs of his lightweight raincloak. "Where the deuce did you come from?" he demanded of Thomas.

"Rowe's Hill, my lord."

Stubbs looked from Richard to the almost belligerent countenance of the footman. "He came with the young mistress," he explained quickly. "And there's no complaint with his service. Indeed—"

But Richard was no longer attending. Brushing both men aside, he hurried up the stairs, nearly colliding with Mrs. Creighton in the hallway. "Where is she?"

"Lady Sherborne? I am sure I don't know, but—"

"Is that plaster I smell? What the devil . . . ?"

Before she could answer, he'd thrown open the door to his bedchamber, to find O'Neal surveying a rather full closet of gowns. "I'd say, milord," the valet murmured, turning around, " 'tis moot, it is, whither to go t' Rowe's Hill like ye were plannin'— by the looks o' it, the lady's here, she is."

It was not as he'd planned it. The decision had been taken from his hands, and as much as he'd wanted to see her, it irritated him that she'd just moved in in his absence. He flung out of the room, stopping only to go to his mother's chamber. And there he found the furniture under holland sheets beneath newly repaired walls as yet half-covered in a soft rose silk. Looking down, he saw the carpet roll, still in its canvas covering, clearly marked "For Lady Sherborne" and bearing the name of an exclusive London rug merchant. Not only had she moved in. She was redoing the place to suit herself! He backed out, now thoroughly furious, having forgotten his earlier intention to do just what she'd done, and retraced his steps back down.

"Thomas!"

"Aye, my lord?"

"Where is she?" Richard demanded grimly.

"Lady Sherborne?"

"Yes."

"As to that, I cannot say to a certainty, my lord."

"Never mind."

He had to think, to calm his temper before he saw her. He was but surprised, that was all, and he'd not considered that she could be at Richlands. He walked slowly, precisely to the library. A little wine, a warm fire, and then he would decide what he would say to her.

The fire blazed, roared almost, from the extra wood that had been piled on it. He unhooked the frogs that held his cloak still and flung the garment over the back of a tall chair near the door. And then he stopped, caught by the sight of a foot barely visible at the side of his favorite leather wing chair in front of the fire.

"Harry?"

The foot moved, shifting the heavy wool shawl that spilled over the arm of the chair, and she came awake with a jolt. He walked purposefully to face her.

"What the devil are you doing here?"

Her chin came up defiantly, and her dark eyes flashed at the tone of his voice. "I believe I have the right!" she retorted.

"I did not give you leave—"

"No, you did not! But then you did not say overmuch when you left either!"

"You deceived me!"

"You left me without so much as an explanation, Richard!" Her voice rose at the remembered hurt and humiliation. "You left but a letter that made not the least sense, and ... and you gave it to Thomas to deliver to me!"

Stung by her anger, he stood over her, his own face reddening. "You deceived me—you plotted this marriage like a damned adventuress. Deny it, Harry!"

"*What*? Oh, 'tis rich, it is! You followed me to Bath, insisting I had no choice but to wed you, and you have the . . . the *cheek* to say I *plotted* to catch you?" she sputtered. " 'Tis outside of enough, my lord!"

"I heard it from your father's lips, Harry! Do not be coming the innocent with me!" The long awaited interview was not going at all as he'd expected. With an effort, he backed off and took a deep breath. "But 'tis water under the bridge now, I daresay, and I own your situation was desperate." Mistaking her outraged silence for attention, he plunged ahead, adding insult to injury. "Given the circumstances, I am prepared to forgive you and accept the marriage."

"Oh, you are, are you?" she asked with deceptive sweetness when at last she found her tongue. "Well, 'tis noble of you, I am sure, but you are quite mistaken if you believe that will suffice. You see, I am not at all prepared to forgive *you*!" Her face flushed, her dark eyes martial now, she disentangled her legs to stand. "You wed me, you got this child of me, and you abandoned me, Richard Standen! You left me to face Hannah's certain scorn, and you went off without so much as a thought to what you had done to me! Six months it has been without so much as a word from you!"

As the shawl fell away, slipping to the floor at her feet, he could only stare, bereft of speech. She was obviously very much with child.

"I . . . Why didn't you tell me, Harry?" he asked, all anger now gone.

"And just how would I have done that? Just where would I have written to you, my lord?" she demanded sarcastically. "Lest you have forgotten, you neglected in your rather terse letter to give me your direction!"

"I didn't know, Harry."

"And you did not care either!" Angry, hurt tears sprang to her eyes and threatened to betray her. While he was still groping for something to say to her, she gathered up her shawl. "I loved you once, Richard," she whispered from the safety of the door. "And you abandoned me."

"Harry!"

But even as he shouted, he heard her run up the stairs. Stunned by what he'd seen and heard, stunned by the knowledge that she would bear his child, he stood rooted to the floor, scarce able to think rationally. And then after the first shock wore off, he was torn between running after her and letting her vent her anger. What could he say? That he was mistaken? That he was sorry? He ran his fingers through his thick black hair distractedly. Guilt warred with raw emotion, tearing at him. If she had not trapped him into the marriage, he'd committed a terrible wrong to her. And even if she had, what he in turn had done was still inexcusable. He closed his eyes, thinking how it must've been for her, faced with her father's anger and Hannah's ridicule. And then for her to have discovered he'd left her with child—how she must hate him now.

"Oh, God, Harry, I'm sorry," he groaned. And then he knew he could not leave it at that—that he had to explain, to ask her forgiveness.

"Harry! Harry!" he yelled, running up the stairs two at a time. "I know I do not bear listening to, but I've got to speak to you! Harry, where the devil are you?"

"Her ladyship has left the house, sir."

He came face-to-face with a strange girl, her blue eyes cold and accusing, blocking the doorway to his chamber. For a moment he hesitated, and then he set her firmly aside.

"Harry!"

"Beggin' yer honor's pardon, but there's Millie there," O'Neal announced, aggrieved, "and she's not wantin' t' give up the field—says she's not budgin' till Lady Sherborne says she ought."

"What?" Still distracted, Richard turned to face his valet, who'd been engaged in fighting his own territorial dispute over the room. "Who in heaven's name is Millie?"

"She is." O'Neal gestured to the girl who now stood martially in the door. "I collect her ladyship's been livin' in your chamber, she has, and the girl—"

"We was movin' soon as t'other chamber's done," Millie interrupted. "We wasn't expectin' ye yet. And we'd a been done afore you come home, but milady's been a trifle indisposed. But it ain't right for him to come here and threaten t' throw her lady-ship's things about!"

" 'Tis his honor's chamber!"

"Let her stay. Tell Mrs. Creighton I'll take one of the guest rooms." Turning back to Millie, Richard asked more reasonably, "Do you know where she went?"

"Out. She was overset, she was, and he—"

"Here now, I was all that was polite t' her, me shrew!" the valet snapped. "But she threw her cloak over her shoulder and left afore I could say scarce a word to 'er, so tell it right if yer bearin' the tale!"

"She was a-weepin'!"

"And I would've helped her, you silly baggage, but between the two o' ye, there was no talkin' to ye!"

"Listen, I did not come up to listen to the both of you brangle, and I've heard enough! Where is 'out'?" Richard demanded.

"Walkin', I'd think—wouldn't you?" she shot back, unrepentant. "Poor soul—and her increasin' and all."

O'Neal met Richard's eyes and sobered. "I collect it did not go like you was a-wishin', yer honor."

"Not at all."

"If 'twas me, I'd leave her be until she feels more th' thing. 'Twas a shock a-seein' ye agin, I'd be bound. Seems t' me—"

"The shock was not all hers," Richard muttered dryly.

"Well, she cannot go far, for 'tis gonna rain, and 'tis gettin' dark, don't ye know? And if yer honor was t' leave her be, I'm thinkin' she might come about, d'ye think?"

"For once you appear to have all the sense in this house, O'Neal," Richard conceded, still trying to cope with the dramatic changes in his plans. "All right, she'll be back before supper surely. Er . . . Millie, is it? Yes, well, when she comes in, send for me."

He walked back downstairs almost in a trance, his mind still troubled, to where he'd first discovered her in his chair. His eyes took in the bright warm blaze in the fireplace, and he recalled how she'd not even been allowed a fire at Rowe's Hill. "She hates me—and with reason," he admitted to himself. Leaving the door open in case she should come back that way, he moved to the sideboard and uncorked the brandy.

Brandishing the bottle in the air, he offered a mocking toast, "To Lady Sherborne! To Richard Standen, bloody foolish bastard that he is!" And then he poured himself a full glass, carried it to the chair, and sat sprawled before the fire, waiting. Slowly, as the brandy warmed him, he allowed himself the luxury of remembering the week that had gained him the child, seeing her again as she had been, recalling the sweetness of discovered passion. There was no help for it, he was caught well and good, in fact and heart. All that had passed since Rowe's Hill was but the floundering.

It did not take him long to discover that he faced the censure of his entire household. Mrs. Creighton moved about sniffing disapprovingly, Stubbs's face was wooden whenever he passed by the door, the maids who ventured in scurried like mice before a cat when they saw him, and even Heloise sat back on her haunches and eyed him as though he were an interloper in his own house.

"I suppose you think me a shallow, callous fellow also," he sighed, leaning down from his chair to pick her up. "And maybe I am, you know, but I'll tell you one thing: I'm going to make it up to her." The cat stared like an owl, its round, unmatched eyes unblinking. "You don't believe me, do you? Well, beginning tomorrow, I'm taking Harry to London. She's going to have the best physician, the best gowns, the best jewelry, the best I can buy her—you hear me, you misbegotten clump of fur?"

Apparently more easily convinced than Harriet, the cat settled down on his lap, stretching across it toward the warmth of the fire. He sat there scratching her ears, drawing comfort from her presence. But it was one thing to confide his dreams to a cat, quite another to explain to his wife.

Nearly half an hour later, he was interrupted from his rather sober musings by Thomas. "What is it? Oh, 'tis you."

"The rest of 'em don't want to tempt your temper, my lord, but I thought perhaps you might wish to know . . ." The footman paused, waiting to make certain he had Lord Sherborne's attention. " 'Tis about the horse, my lord."

"What horse?" Richard roused himself,

straightening in his chair, sensing it was a matter of some import. "Two Harry? Tell Cates to tend to it."

" 'Tis Cates who told Stubbs," Thomas persisted stubbornly. "But he could not stop the mistress."

An awful premonition washed over him. "Couldn't stop her from what? Out with it, man! Where is she?"

"Beggin' your pardon, my lord, but she took the horse."

He lurched to his feet, nearly oversetting the chair.

"The deuce she did! And he let her? In her condition? Of all the cork-brained . . . the stupid . . . Dash it, Thomas, but she cannot ride! And Two Harry's not a lady's mount!" Already halfway to the door, he flung back over his shoulder, "When? When did she leave?"

"That, my lord, you'll have to ask Mr. Cates. I did but think you'd wish to hear the horse was missing."

"Stubbs! Stubbs! Where's Cates? He cannot have been such a fool as to let her take Two Harry! Dammit, where is everybody? Set up a search party! Tell Cates I'll have his head if anything's happened to her!"

He tore through the house as though possessed, leaving Thomas to shake his head. "He wouldn't look for her, but he'll search for the animal," he muttered.

Despite the lateness of the day, every available man was sent out, with Richard taking the lead of one party. At first the air was merely misty, but as the sun set, it began to drizzle steadily, soaking through the searchers' clothes. After nearly two hours of combing along lanes and hedgerows, Richard had to admit she must've taken shelter somewhere. Relucantly he turned back, telling himself that she was all right, that she'd probably doubled back to the house when it got dark, that they'd but been on the proverbial wild-goose chase.

"She's back?" he asked Mrs. Creighton as he removed his dripping cloak.

"If she is, I am sure I haven't seen her," the housekeeper sniffed. "And Cook is holding supper."

"Mrs. Creighton, has she any friends in the neighborhood—anyone she visits or who visits here?"

Rivulets ran from his wet, plastered hair to stream down his face, and it was obvious that he was chilled to the bone. But she could see he was truly worried, and she relented slightly, shaking her head.

"There's none I can think of. She busied herself here most of the time, except when she went to London, of course, and other than the tradesmen and the riding instructor from Tetwell, who does not come anymore, I cannot think she knew anyone. She has not been feeling quite the thing lately," she added significantly.

"She never paid calls?"

"No."

"Stubbs?"

"No."

"Well, she cannot have gone far," he rationalized, trying to tell himself that she had to be all right. "Ten to one, she's sought shelter. If she's not back in another hour, we'll take the lanterns out and try again."

17

She gave the horse its head, letting it run a half-mile or so, heedless of the fact that riding astride exposed her lower legs. It didn't matter anyway, for her attempts at being a grand lady had come to naught. The misty rain cooled her bitter, painful anger slowly, and as she reined Two Harry to a walk, that anger was replaced by despair. Richard's homecoming had not been as she'd planned it. For months she'd dreamed of his returning to find her, not asleep in a chair, but rather as mistress of his house, exquisitely gowned and coiffed, presiding elegantly over dinner, exhibiting all those qualities she'd striven so hard to achieve in the six months past. Instead, he'd discovered an ungainly, plain woman far gone with child. In the fantasies of her mind, she'd expected him to be surprised, pleased even, and eager to make amends, she supposed. But it hadn't happened. Far from pleasing him, her presence had angered him, and the hurt she felt again was almost too much to bear.

She had no notion of how far she'd ridden when at last she realized she was very cold and it was nearly dark. Turning back, she feared herself lost, and she doubted Two Harry knew the way either. It was all of a piece, after all, another thing she'd done wrong. But as darkness descended like a blanket over the hilly, tree-covered countryside, and the rain came down harder, she reached the familiar road from London. Spurring Two Harry lightly, she urged him onto the well-traveled carriage lanes.

Well, Richard might be displeased, angry even, to have her at Richlands, but he could scarce want to cast himself in the terrible light of having thrust her out. And surely he would want the child, for had he not said he wanted children? Recalling again her mother's adage about spilt milk, she resolutely determined to attempt a reasonable accommodation with him: she would offer not to interfere with his life in exchange for his recognizing her position and his heir. And later, after the babe was born, she'd try again to be fashionable and elegant, perhaps even going so far as to set up an establishment in London.

The rain came down in sheets now, soaking her cloak and the gown beneath. Shivering from the cold, she saw the road diverge toward Richlands. The horse plodded, his hooves sinking in the muddy mire of the lane through Richlands' park. Her cropped hair dripped, then streamed, nearly blinding her, and her hands were almost too cold to hold the reins. Ahead in the distance, barely visible, was the faint glow of lights from the house. Thinking to cross the field rather than follow the winding road, she nudged Two Harry toward the hedgerow.

He balked, unwilling to jump even the low thicket, and she, thinking he needed a run at it, pulled back. He reared, nearly unseating her, but she held on.

"Come on, we are nearly there!" she urged him through the now driving rain. Spurring once again, she headed him for the field.

He ran straight, gaining speed, but unused to jumping, stumbled against rather than cleared the row. For an awful moment she rose in the saddle, caught her foot briefly in the stirrup, and pitched forward as she and Two Harry went down. And her last thought before she hit the ground was that she'd destroyed Richard's horse. Then the pain of impact was followed by oblivion.

She revived slowly, conscious first of the pain in her back and then of the almost numbing cold. She was sprawled, her face turned from the wet grass and mud, her arms embracing the ground. And she could not move as the deep ache in her back spread forward, clutching her abdomen, tearing at her with such intensity that she could not breathe. She tried to scream, but the pain was so fierce that she could not hear herself. She was going to die undiscovered in the mud and rain.

Unable to eat, Richard paced before the waning fire, alternating between reassuring himself she'd taken shelter and the fear that she was still out somewhere in the rain. Already another search party was forming in the drive, but he didn't have much hope for it. Resolutely he warmed his hands one last time and reached for the dry wool cloak O'Neal had found for him.

He was brought up short by the sound of shouts outside, and he allowed himself to think she'd come home. But before he could reach the door, Thomas burst in.

"The horse is back, my lord, and by the looks of it, 'tis trouble for the mistress!"

Pulling his cloak about him, Richard ran out as Cates held a lantern to Two Harry, examining him. "He's taken a tumble, my lord," the trainer noted, bending down to feel the animal's forelegs. " 'Tis knee-deep in mire he's been, but naught's broken."

But Richard's eyes were on the muddy saddle. "Never mind the horse," he heard himself say, his voice strangely odd. He was in a nightmare.

"By the looks o' it, she's been thrown," O'Neal murmured behind him.

"Aye." Richard ran his hands over the wet saddle with sinking heart. "Get the rest of the lanterns. There's grass and brush in the stirrup, so 'tis the fields."

" 'Tis too dark," someone mumbled.

"My lord—"

"We're going to cover every foot of ground between here and the main road, d'you hear me? Simpson, you will go with Ames . . . Collins, you take Blake . . . Keighley, follow Edwards and Robbins! And—"

"I'd go with you, my lord," Thomas interrupted curtly.

"Beggin' yer honor's honor, but I'd go with ye also," O'Neal decided.

"You?" Richard's eyebrow lifted. "All right. Stubbs, you will tell Mrs. Creighton to warm the bed and have a fire laid for Lady Sherborne—and send Wilcox for Dr. Paxton."

Realistically, he knew they had not much chance of finding her in the dark and the rain, but he had to try. By first light of morning, she could well be dead from the cold. Pulling his cloak even tighter against the wet wind, he shouted, "Release the dogs!" and swung up into his saddle.

They divided, most of them fanning out over the park, their lanterns bobbing and glowing, illuminating the raindrops that slanted toward the earth. Richard, waving to O'Neal and Thomas to follow him, headed for the London road. He'd ride all the way out, then come back toward the house, crossing the fields between the turnoff and the park, praying that somehow he'd find her. But in the darkness and the mire, he could pass within yards of her and never know it. And that thought was even more chilling than the cold wind that cut through his cloak.

The ride was tedious, hampered by the water in the carriage tracks and the sodden turf, and the silence was broken only by the sound of the two hunting dogs sniffing and bugling and of the pelting drops that splashed in the ruts. Forcing his thoughts to the present, denying himself any reflection now, Richard strained to listen, hoping that she might hear the dogs and call out. From time to time he rose in his stirrups to shout, "Harry! Harry! Harrrrryyy!" And each time, his words seemed to disappear into the blackness and die.

"My lord, there's somethin' over there!" Thomas shouted, spurring his horse toward a shape that moved along the ridge of a hill. And then he called back, "Nay, 'tis naught but a dead branch blowin'!"

After several such missteps, all three men were disheartened. They'd ridden nigh two hours, and with each passing minute it seemed less like they'd find her. Finally Richard turned to Thomas. "You and O'Neal go back and warm yourselves. If there's any word of her, send someone back to me."

"And you?"

Richard gestured in the direction of the house. "I mean to take Molly and cut across this last field. You take Samson back with you." He stood in his saddle once more and peered grimly into the blackness. "Maybe with but one dog to bark, I can hear something."

"And if you honor's horse was t' stumble . . ." O'Neal shook his head. ". . . tomorrow 'tis you we're lookin' for."

"I am not c-cold, my lord," Thomas maintained stoutly, despite the decided shiver of his hunched shoulders.

"No—go on, both of you," Richard ordered. "Send word if any of the others have found her."

He reined in and waited. Finally O'Neal sighed and reached across to Thomas' reins. "Come on, me boy, 'tis bound and determined to wallow in guilt he is. Thinks if he was to make himself sick, 'twould be justice."

"One of these days I shall turn you off, and you'll have to learn your place as a valet," Richard growled.

There was no question about it—he wanted to be left alone. He waited until they were about a hundred feet away before he turned toward the hedgerow, thinking to follow it to the next field and then back across.

"Come on, Molly," he murmured, more for himself than for the dog. "We're not done."

The hound, which had lain down beside his horse's feet, lurched upward when he clicked the reins. Moving ahead, she sniffed along the tight, dense hedge, jumping game. Birds and rabbits flapped and scattered. And then Molly dropped her back haunches slightly and howled.

"Molly! Not now!"

But she wouldn't budge, not even when he rode a few yards on down the row. Disgusted, he came back, thinking to leash her, and dismounted. But as he held the lantern up, he could see the piece of sodden cloth caught in the brambles where it had torn.

"Harry! Harry!"

There was no answer other than the rustling of dying leaves in the wind. He bent to buckle the leash onto the collar and pull the dog away, when Molly edged closer to the hedge, pushing her nose under it, whining.

"Ten to one, 'tis naught but something you think I'd like to shoot," he muttered, leaving her to remount his horse. Then, moving back to give the animal room, he took a run at the hedge several feet down from where the dog still lay, and cleared it easily.

"Oh, God . . . Harry! O'Neal! Thomas! Over here!" He yelled for them so loudly that his lungs felt raw. "Over here!"

Sliding down from his saddle, he knelt at the sodden tangle of body and clothing, his heart pounding in his throat, his mind terrified of what he'd found. Her eyes were closed, her skin wet and cold and muddy where he touched her face, and for one awful moment he thought she was dead.

"Harry . . ." He worked frantically, lifting her, rubbing her face with his hands, trying to warm her cold body. "Harry, you are found!" he cried, cradling her against him. Tears rolled, mingled with the rain, and slid off his cheeks. "Oh, God, Harry, I came back for you . . . I did not want . . ."

O'Neal dismounted and walked over to lay a hand on his shoulder. "Here, now, yer honor—there's not the time," he murmured gruffly.

Richard slid his hand along the slick mud, feeling her neck and finding the thready pulse. And then he began working in earnest, chafing her hands with his. Looking up at the valet, he managed to choke out, "She's alive."

Thomas brought his lantern closer, holding it to her ashen face. "We've got to get her inside, my lord."

Nodding, Richard rose to his knees, still holding her, and slid his soaked cloak off his shoulders. "I'll lift her, and you try to wrap this around her—'tisn't dry, but it's warmer from being on me.''

"I dunno if we should move her."

" 'Twould take an hour and more by the time you rode back to the house, got blankets and oiled cloth, and came back. And that's not to say that we could get a carriage in here. No, we've got to move her.''

It was like wrapping deadweight, but the two servants managed to get the cloak around her, with O'Neal muttering, " 'Tis yer honor that'll take sick too, don't ye know?''

"Do you think you can hand her up—between the two of you, I mean?''

Somehow they managed. Richard remounted, and the Irishman and Thomas lifted and pushed until they had her in his arms. Then, with O'Neal leading his horse, Richard held her against him, curving his back to shelter her from the wind.

"Praise God you have found her!" Mrs. Creighton breathed as Richard carried Harriet into the house. And then, peering more closely, she gasped, "Oh, my!''

There, beneath the blazing light from the entrance-hall chandelier, Richard looked down and realized that the pool forming on the floor wasn't entirely water. The hem of the gown that hung beneath his sodden cloak dripped blood.

The doctor, emerging from Richard's library, where he'd waited with a glass of heated punch, took one look at the inert form in the viscount's arms and went into action. "Put her to bed, and roll a blanket beneath her. Have someone bring a basin and water. I'll need laudanum if she wakes." One after the other, he issued terse orders as he followed Richard up the stairs. He needed towels, he needed a warming pan for the bed, he needed someone to be ready to hold her down if the need arose.

"Do you think she'll be all right?" Richard asked anxiously as he laid her across the folded blanket that Millie thrust into the bed.

"Haven't looked at her yet," Paxton snapped. "If anything's certain, though, 'tis that she's going to lose the child. As for the rest, I'll just have to see."

18 Paxton came out briefly to report on what he'd discovered. Richard, still in wet clothes, paced the carpeted hallway, a glass of the heated punch in his hand.

"Well, naught's broken that I can tell—'course, 'tis early times yet, and I don't know about the back. Ankle's badly sprained where it twisted when she fell. And she'll be fortunate if she don't contract a lung inflammation from this."

"But she *will* be all right?"

"Hard to say at this juncture—have to wait and see."

With that, the physician disappeared back inside, leaving Richard to worry about countless imagined dangers. Another hour passed before O'Neal was able to persuade him to bathe and change into dry clothing. But as Mrs. Creighton had just emerged to bustle past him down the stairs, brushing aside his questions with impatience, there seemed to be little else to do. All he'd gotten out of Creighton was " 'Twill be a long night, I fear."

"But has she awakened?" he'd asked.

"Now and again, but between the laudanum and the pain, she's not knowing anything," was the short reply.

Finally, most of the household went to bed, leaving him to remove downstairs to his library, where he tried to drink a brandy and read. But his powers of concentration were gone. He threw another large log on the fire himself and thought he'd never again be warm. But that was, he admitted freely, nothing to what must be happening to Harry.

Dawn filtered through the many-paned windows, bathing the room with an unnatural rosy glow. The silence was broken only by the steady ticking of the clock on the mantel, a ticking that seemed suddenly overloud. And still there was no word from above, nothing but the occasional shuffling of tired footsteps.

The clock read twenty minutes past the hour of six. For eight hours and more, he'd been left to wonder and worry, and there seemed no end to it. All manner of things went through his mind, not the least of which was guilt. Like everything else she'd faced in the fourteen years he'd known her, Harry faced this alone also.

"My lord?"

His heart rose into his throat until he realized it was Thomas. The footman was still buttoning his coat, and he looked as though he'd not slept either.

"O'Neal asked me t' tell you to come up."

Hope flared briefly, but the somberness of Thomas' voice dashed it. "Is there a change then?" Richard wanted to know.

"As to that, I'd not say, for I wasn't told. But I believe you were asked for."

Despite the heavy thudding of his heart and the sickening dread that knotted his stomach, Richard climbed the stairs quickly, pausing to knock at the chamber door. As if expecting him, the doctor stepped outside and into the hallway. His voice low, he moved close to Richard and explained, "The babe was born an hour ago, my lord, but I saw no reason to wake you, for it did not, could not live, and the struggle was to save your wife. She bled copiously, I am afraid, and I—"

"No! I'll not believe it! 'Tis not right!" Richard choked in anguish. "Harry—"

"She has the will, but—"

"Ten thousand pounds and she lives . . . Anything . . ." he offered desperately. "Send to London, anywhere . . ."

"My lord," Paxton cut in tiredly, "if you would but let me speak, I pray you. 'Tis in the hands of God now, not mine. The hemorrhage has lessened, the afterbirth appeared normal and intact, but I know not if she has the strength to survive. What I could say to you is that I have done my best and there's naught else to do—money is meaningless now."

"Then you are telling me she dies," Richard decided heavily. "You are telling me she is too weak to live."

"I am telling you I do not know."

"Knighton—"

"Would tell you the same, I fear—as would any reputable physician. Were I you, I should pray."

"Is she conscious? I'd see her."

"She lapses between sleep and wakefulness, is often confused from the laudanum, and she does not ask for you. In this case, I should not recommend it."

It was as though numbness descended with the doctor's words, and Richard, too stunned to speak, turned and walked slowly down the hall. Having practiced his religion much as any other buck of the *ton*, he was not even certain of his standing with the Almighty. Reaching the chamber he'd taken, he slumped into a chair and tried to compose his thoughts. Any of the prayers of his childhood seemed woefully inadequate, and after a brief review he simply began to talk to God. It was not right that she should die before she'd truly lived. It was not right that it should happen now, not now that he'd come home to her. Much of her life, she'd been lonely and neglected; she must not leave this world feeling so now.

His fervent thoughts were interrupted by the slight thump of Athena landing on his leg. For a moment he started to brush her off, to tell her to go away, and then he recalled just how much Harry's cats had meant to her. His arms closed convulsively about the tabby, holding it close. It struggled to stand on its hind legs, reaching to lick at his face, cleaning up the tears that flowed unnoted.

Harry must not leave this world feeling alone and neglected . . . Harry must not leave this world feeling alone. Lifting the cat off, he lurched from his chair and hurried back down the hall. She wasn't alone, and he meant to make her know it. She wasn't going to die alone.

The room was as silent as a tomb when he slipped into it. Mrs. Creighton and Millie dozed in chairs near the bed, and Dr. Paxton moved about noiselessly, cleaning the instruments of delivery. The body of the infant, washed and swaddled in fresh linen, lay in a basket just inside the door. Richard stopped momentarily and stood staring down into the still, tiny face. Its skin was so thin, parchmentlike, and its head no bigger than a child's fist. The deep imprint of forceps marred an otherwise perfectly formed face.

Paxton looked up briefly. "It was a boy. He did not survive the fall."

He'd always wanted a son, but now that wanting paled beside the fear that he'd lose Harry also.

Drawing away from the child he'd gotten of her, he turned to the great four-postered bed, unprepared for the sight of her. She was pale and bloodless, her skin as alabaster as a statue, and she was so still, so motionless, that his breath caught. Her cropped brown hair curled in wild disarray, her eyes were but dark shadows beneath their lids, and her face was utterly devoid of expression. For a moment he thought he'd come too late, but then, beneath the arm that crossed her breast, he could see the gentle rise and fall of her chest. She looked so small lying there, not much larger than a child, or so it seemed.

"Harry."

He dropped down to sit on the bed beside her, and reached to possess himself of one of her cold hands. Rubbing it gently between his own, chafing it as though he could somehow infuse her with his own warmth, he leaned closer.

"Harry."

" 'Tis doubtful she can hear you, my lord," he heard Paxton say.

Ignoring the doctor, ignoring the two women who still slept a few feet away, Richard tightened his clasp on her hand and spoke low and evenly to her. "Harry, whether you hear me or no, there's much that I mean to tell you. Did you know that I can still remember the first time I saw you? You were but a little girl—though we were of an age, you did not quite reach my shoulder. And you were wearing a white dress with a pink sash, as I recall it. 'Twas when my aunt wed your father. I doubt you could forget that. And I remember your first words to me when I said we were to be related—you said you did not mind me, but you'd as lief not have Hannah.

"But do you know what I think of most when I think of then, Harry? You were such a lively, taking little thing. Do you remember climbing that tree so that I would not find you? Do you remember winning my father's watch fob by daring to cross Rowe's Ford? You were game for anything, as I recall. And even though you warned me about your papa's bull, you followed me into the field anyway. I thought we were both going to die that day. But as it was, you were birched for knowing better, and I was excused. And your papa would not listen to you or me in the matter. I think 'twas then that you began to change. Oh, it was slowly at first, and then with each passing year you were quieter and quieter, until I'd begun to think Hannah had taken all your spirit from you."

He talked on, droning almost, speaking of things long past, recounting almost everything he ever knew of her, all the way to their ownership of Two Harry, and their brief marriage, talking until he was hoarse. "I guess what I am asking, Harry," he said finally, "is that you become that child once again, that you learn to live before you die." His voice broke. "I'd like to say 'tis my unselfish self that speaks, but 'tis not. I don't know whether it came from the fear that I might lose you, but I have learned much these past hours. Harry, I love you, and I don't want to let you go. I want to begin anew with you. I don't care about why we wed, I don't care about Hannah or Uncle John. I don't care about Two Harry or anything else. I just don't ever want you to be alone again—I want to be there with you."

"My lord—"

"Oh, God, Harry, can you not hear me at all?" Richard groaned as Dr. Paxton pulled him back.

"You've got to leave her be, my lord. 'Tis only rest and a cessation of the bleeding that will give her strength."

"I'd stay."

"You are but in the way," Paxton insisted firmly.

Then, speaking more kindly, he added, "But I will send for you as soon as anything changes—for good or ill."

"I'd have her know I am here."

"She cannot know it, my lord. The laudanum makes her sleep deeply."

Richard hesitated, loath to leave and yet unwilling to do anything to harm her chances of survival. Paxton, taking advantage of his emotional exhaustion, pressed the matter. "If you would be of any use to Lady Sherborne, you should seek your own bed. If she improves, there is still the matter of her injuries, and the healing of body and mind will come slowly. You are more needed then."

Standing, Richard ran his fingers through his hair, combing it as though that would somehow revive him. "All right," he sighed finally. "But you will send for me."

"Of a certainty."

As he passed her, Mrs. Creighton's eyes squeezed shut, but not before he saw the tears that streamed down her cheeks. Millie, on the other hand, stared up, stricken.

"Oh, sir, 'tis sorry I am. I thought ye didn't have a care fer her," she whispered.

"Why would you?" he managed back.

He sought his bed then and tried to sleep despite the lightness of the room, but sleep wouldn't come. From time to time O'Neal came in, went silently about his business, and retreated. Finally Richard whiled away the hours by planning for Harriet's recuperation. He'd take her to London, have her dressed by the finest modistes, present her to the *ton*, and give her all the things that Hannah had made her miss. By late afternoon he finally dozed.

"Faith, and she's awake, or so they tell me,"

O'Neal murmured as he shook his master. "Old Friday Face wasn't wantin' me to wake ye, but I knew ye'd want t' know."

"Huh?" Richard shook his head and rubbed at his full day's growth of black beard. His body ached and his mouth tasted like Napoleon's army had marched through it. "What time is it?" he asked, sitting up.

"Nigh six."

Somehow it did not seem possible, and before he allowed himself to believe it, he wanted to be certain he did not dream.

"Lud. But she's awake?"

"Aye."

Unbelievable relief washed over him. He was to have another chance at happiness, another chance to love her as she ought to be loved. His heart in his throat, he could not help wanting to know, "Did she ask for me?"

The valet shifted uncomfortably and looked away. "Nay, but who's t' say 'twasn't an oversight, I ask ye? What wi' the nasty fall and all—faith, and I'd be surprised she's thinkin' any." Then, raising troubled eyes, the young Irishman sobered completely. " 'Tis sorry I am about the babe, milord."

His hopes, so lately risen, plummeted now, but the pain Richard felt was not as much for the babe as for the fact that Harriet did not want to see him. That he'd bared his soul for naught.

19 The wind howled, carrying sheets of rain that sprayed the dead leaves like shot, echoing eerily through the family graveyard. The water swirled at the feet of the small group gathered to witness the interment. The vicar, come to Richlands for the sad ceremony, spoke but briefly, his words for the most part carried away on the wind. And then the little casket was slid into the opening inside the Standen vault as tiny Henry James Standen joined three generations of his ancestors.

Henry James Standen. It had been left to Richard to choose what name, if any, the infant carried to eternity, for Harriet was far too ill to discuss the matter. Well, "Henry" was appropriate, he decided, since both his father and his son had been killed in falls from horses. And both needlessly. But where the elder Henry had known what he risked, the babe was but an innocent victim. For that Richard blamed himself. If he'd not forced the stupid, foolish quarrel on Harriet, she'd not have stormed from the house.

"Faith, and ye'll take sick yerself, milord," O'Neal chided him, laying a hand on Richard's shoulder. "And then ye'd be no good t' her, now, would ye? I'm thinkin' 'tis only yerself that can aid her mend."

But Richard had begun to doubt that. Ever since

she'd regained consciousness, Harry had done
naught but stare at the wall when he attempted to
talk with her. Telling her she'd lost the child had
been but the worst of it, for then she'd turned away,
dry-eyed, unable to cry even. How she must hate
him now. Her last words before the accident still
haunted him, and probably would forever. *I loved
you once . . . you abandoned me.* And the irony of it
all was not lost on him: he, Richard Standen, buck
of the *ton*, had realized he loved his wife too late.

Squaring his shoulders, he nodded. "I suppose I'll
have to let her know 'tis over."

"Aye."

The loss of the child and the illness of the young
mistress cast a pall over the entire household. As
he trod the stairs to see Harriet, Richard thought
the hushed silence almost more than he could bear.
Had it not been for an occasional brangle over who
took precedence in the ordering of things upstairs
between O'Neal and Millie, there'd have been no
noise at all. As it was, they'd even reached a sort
of truce in the three days since he'd returned to
Richlands.

"Harry?"

She was lying, her back toward him, facing the
wall, and he couldn't tell if she were awake or
asleep. Dropping into a chair beside the bed, he
reached to touch her shoulder. Rubbing his fingers
gently over the bony ridge, he leaned forward to
talk.

"Can you hear me?"

Stony silence.

"Harry, 'tis done. The Reverend Mr. Wilcox came
over from St. John's and spoke, and Mrs. Tilford
in the village made him a dress, and . . ." His voice
broke for a moment, and then he recovered. "I
named him Henry for my father, Harry, and James

for your grandfather. I did not think you would wish it to be John, you know." His hand closed more tightly on her shoulder, and his eyes closed. Swallowing hard, he tried to go on, but faltered. "Oh, God, Harry, I know not what to say. I'd give anything if—"

"It was not your fault," she whispered almost inaudibly.

"I wish I had known—I would have done things differently, believe me."

She closed her eyes and clenched her fists, stiffening beneath his hand.

"Harry . . ." Her silence was more devastating than anything she could have flung at him. Finally he released her shoulder and leaned back. "Do you hurt? Are you in pain? Would you have Dr. Paxton?" But there was no answer from the bed. "I'll get him," he sighed, rising in defeat.

She heard the door close behind him, and all rigidity left her. Stifling a sob with her knuckle between her teeth, she rolled into a ball. "I hurt, but you cannot know how much," she whispered again.

Through her folly, she'd lost her child, and it did not seem right that she had lived. And Richard's kindness now was that of guilt or pity, she was certain. Well, she did not want his pity—she'd not wanted it then and she did not want it now. If he could not love her—and after what had happened, she knew he could not—well, then there was naught else to be said. Besides, she had a surfeit of her own guilt and self-pity, and did not need any more.

All she'd done had been for naught—the coming to Richlands, the learning to run his house, the new clothes, and the babe. But it was the babe that hurt the most. At first, when Dr. Paxton had told her she carried it, she'd considered it one of life's cruel jests, but then as it grew within her, it had become a child to love. And she'd dreamed of it, cherished it, and planned for it. And she'd lost it.

"Lady Sherborne?"

"Yes."

"Lord Sherborne believes you in pain." The doctor pulled the chair Richard had used closer and peered into her face. "Where does it hurt? The ankle . . . the back . . . or your lower limbs?" But even as he spoke, he held out the cup. "I have mixed some laudanum to ease you."

"No."

"Even though I do not think you have broken any bones, you have sustained bruises and sprains sufficient to cause you distress for some time. And you are very weak."

"My child is dead," she said simply.

"Laudanum, dear lady, will ease mind and body whilst you heal." He waited for her to struggle up and then he held the cup for her. "Though you do not think it now, you are young and this will pass. And had it not been for the unfortunate accident, the birth would have been perfectly ordinary, so you must not despair of another child."

"Two Harry?" she asked dully. "Is Two Harry dead also?"

He was surprised by her interest in the animal that had nearly caused her death. "The horse? No, not at all."

"Then perhaps he will forgive me that which I cannot forgive myself." She lay back weakly and turned her head away. "I should rather have that than false love."

Richard met the doctor when he came out. "Did she speak to you? Were you able to ease her?"

"I gave her laudanum to make her sleep. Time, my lord—'tis time she will need." And then Paxton shook his head. "Poor lady—she asked of the horse. Other than that, her mind wanders, I fear."

"I cannot like opiates," Richard murmured.

"They soothe like naught else. Perhaps your lordship—"

"No. The sooner she is weaned from it, the better, I should think." Then, almost by afterthought, he added, "You can tell her, should she ask again, that she need not worry for the horse."

As the doctor turned back to tend his patient, Richard continued on down the hall. He ought to do something about Two Harry, he supposed, but he couldn't bring himself to even look at the animal since the accident. The pride and pleasure Two Harry had given him was gone, lost in a soggy, bloody field.

To Harriet, the month following her baby's death was but a blur. Lost in her own mourning and drugged with laudanum whenever she waked, she slowly began to accept it, but she still could not face Richard. Hurt and guilt intermingled to make even the smallest discourse painful. Even as he sat patiently beside the bed, telling her of this and that, she knew in her heart that he did not want her, that he had to blame her for the death of his heir, that his kindness was but his own guilt over leaving her. But she endured his attempts at conversation as punishment for what she had done.

"Are you still hurting?" he asked one day when she was feeling particularly uncommunicative.

"No."

"Then you will have to rise from your bed, Harry, else you'll not regain your strength. If you are up to it, I should like to bundle you into the carriage and take you for a drive out in the air."

"I don't—"

"Then at least attempt to walk in the park with me," he coaxed. " 'Tis brisk, but if you are warmly clad—"

"I think I should rather read, Richard, and perhaps nap."

"No. I'll not leave you up here to dose yourself with an opiate again, Harry," he told her flatly, his blue eyes meeting hers, his expression sober. "I had Millie throw out the bottle this morning. Now, if you truly would read, I'll help you downstairs and we can sit in the library. You need to be up, Harry, else you'll not mend."

She wanted to scream at him that she'd never mend anyway, but she doubted he would understand. Instead, she looked away. "All right."

"The park, the road, or the library?"

"It does not matter."

Her apathetic response was daunting, but he wasn't letting her retreat within her self-pity again. "Alas, Lady Sherborne, if you will not choose, then you'd best not complain. We shall take a walk then, and if you become too tired, you may lean on me."

She knew he was doing it because he was irrevocably tied to her, and he had no use for an invalid wife. But it didn't matter. If he wished to walk, she'd walk, and then he would leave her be.

"All right."

To her discomfort, he remained in the room while Millie and Alice dressed her and brushed her hair. The gown hung on her, a reminder of how much weight she'd lost. She weaved slightly and wished for the laudanum. "Perhaps a few drops . . ."

"No. I have told Paxton that I think the stuff robs you of your mind, Harry," he answered quietly. "What you need are food and air."

She moved stiffly, nearly falling twice on the

stairs, but he kept a firm grip on her arm, supporting her. At the bottom, he stopped to pull her cloak closer over her pelisse. "With two outdoor garments, you shouldn't be too cold, do you think?" His fingers worked the frogs, then straightened her bonnet, tying it beneath her chin.

He was right: it was chilly. The damp November air hit her face and turned her breath to steam. And the turf of the park in front of the house was soft and springy as her soft kid shoes trod over it. But it all smelled fresh rather than musty, and the air was invigorating. For a moment she forgot her misery, forgot that beneath his civil facade he must hate her, and she breathed deeply of the cold fresh air.

"The trees are bare, of course, and the grass more than half brown, but there is still a barren beauty to the place, I think," he murmured conversationally, drawing her hand into the crook of his elbow. "But then I must suppose you have explored the place when you first arrived."

"No. I had not the time." Then, surprising herself, she unbent to add, "Your Creighton and Stubbs were rather daunting, you know, and it took a full month ere they would accept I had the right to tell them anything."

"I found your lists, Harry."

"Oh."

"No, actually I was impressed. I should never have thought to go about it that way, but it was very effective. 'Billy Mills—mucks out the stables and tends the horses; Will Gannett—repairs tack and the vehicles; Johnny Johnson—trains the animals, has ill wife, Mary, and two small sons; Betty Sims—tweeny, an orphan; Martha Green—' "

"Stop it,' she protested, embarrassed.

"You know, until I found your lists, I had no

notion I employed so many people here." He stopped walking and turned to face her. "There's not been one of them who has not come to inquire about you these past several weeks, Harry."

" 'Twas kind of them."

"And that's not to mention the tenants. Did you realize that Bertha Gray has sent two puddings and a loaf of currant bread? Or that little Sammy Smith has brought me no fewer than six dead rabbits 'for the mistress, yer unnerstan'—thought mebbe 'er could 'ave a pasty of 'em'?" he mimicked the boy's manner. "The tenants have dashed near fed the household staff while you have been ill, my dear."

"Mrs. Gray could not afford it, Richard—you will have to see she is paid."

"Me? I shouldn't like to insult her, Harry. *You'll* have to see what can be done in the matter."

"I . . ." She shook her head and dug in the soft, damp earth with the toe of her shoe. "I don't think so."

"Harry . . ." He spoke gently, softly, and there was a coaxing inflection in the word. "As cold as you must think me to say it, life does commence whether we wish to go with it or not. And so long as we are here, we must continue with the business of living. Whether you wish it or no, we are wed, and we have to reach an agreement as to—"

"Can you not leave me alone?" she cried, bursting into tears. "You left me. Why did you come back?" Then, before he could stop her, she'd turned and started back for the house, stumbling as she tried to run.

He stood, stunned as stone, until he saw her fall. And then he ran after her, reaching her as she struggled to her feet. "Silly goose! You have not your strength for that! You've got to tread lightly until you are well, Harry." He caught at her hands, examining them. " 'Tis just mud," he muttered, relieved. His arm slid under hers, supporting her. "Come on, we'd best get back before you are chilled to the marrow."

Much later, after she'd returned to her bed, he sat at his desk and considered what could be done for her. And slowly, ever so slowly, he determined a plan to woo his wife back to living, back to loving him. Even if he had to prod her unmercifully, he was going to make her care again.

His mind decided, he trod the steps up to the guest chamber, stopping briefly to tell Millie, "Since Lady Sherborne is no longer to be drugged on laudanum, tell her I shall expect her at dinner. And see to it that she wears something fetching, will you?"

A conspiratorial smile spread over the girl's face. "Of a certainty, milord. And shall I tell her ye'll be needin' yer own chamber also?"

"Do you think she is up to the move?"

"Well, 'twould give her somethin' t' do besides grievin', wouldn't it?" the little maid reasoned. "But don't ye fret none, for me and Mr. O'Neal'll see to it."

"Millie . . ." For a moment he hesitated, well aware of the gap between master and servant, and then he sighed. " 'Twill not be an easy task, I fear, but I mean to make Lady Sherborne go about more. I do not want her sitting blue-deviled in her room. Do you understand me? When she complains of things, I don't want you to sympathize with her any more than absolutely necessary."

"Beggin' yer pardon?"

"I'd rather endure her fury than her apathy."

A glint of understanding brightened the girl's eyes. "I was a-wonderin' how long ye meant to let old Paxton make her ladyship into an invalid. 'Tis right glad I am ye mean to do somethin' about it."

20

"Let me not to the marriage of true minds
Admit impediments. Love is not love
Which alters when it alteration finds,
Or bends with the remover to remove ...

"Richard, I don't wish to read any more of this," Harriet muttered in exasperation.

" 'Tis my favorite of the sonnets, Harry."

"Then you read it," she snapped.

"I like the sound of your voice. Please."

Eyeing him almost malevolently over the top of the thin volume of Shakespeare, she sighed. "And I suppose if I will not, you will devise yet another scheme for my entertainment, won't you?"

"We could play whist if you prefer."

"I am heartily sick of whist."

"Or we could walk outside in the fresh air," he offered, trying not to smile at her restiveness.

"Did you never think I should like to be alone?" she demanded peevishly. "That I should become tired of the constant employment of my mind?"

"No. Go on—you are about to the part of this one that I like," he coaxed. "You read quite well, you know."

"Richard, I never knew you to like literature in your life."

"Ah, but then you saw me only as a grubby, scapegrace cousin come to get you into all manner of pranks when we were children, and then as an infrequent visitor when we were grown. I like all manner of things, Harry. In fact, I had just been thinking that perhaps you would enjoy the *Iliad*."

"Were *you* planning to read it out loud?" she asked with deceptive sweetness. "For I assure you I am not. For two weeks—two weeks, Richard—you have done naught but plague me to read to you and entertain you. And when I have refused, you have taken it upon yourself to entertain me. I am not a child to be amused, you know."

"I believe we were about to the spot where old Will waxed eloquent on the nature of love, Harry. Do go on."

"'O, no! it is an ever fixèd mark,'" she read, then stopped to look at him again. "Must I?"

"'Twould please me greatly."

She eyed him with disfavor and sighed expressively before continuing:

> "That looks on tempests and is never shaken;
> It is the star to every wandering bark,
> Whose worth's unknown, although his height
>   be taken.
> Love's not Time's fool, though rosy lips
>   and cheeks
> Within his bending sickle's compass come;
> Love alters not with his brief hours and weeks,
> But bears it out even to the edge of doom.
> If this be error, and upon me proved,
> I never writ, nor man ever loved."

Laying aside the book, she stared for a moment into the flickering flames in the fireplace. "'Tis obvious that Shakespeare wrote this for a lady rather than for the truth of it," she declared flatly. "What fustian!"

"I collect you are ready for a hand of whist, then."

"I must surely owe you a year's allowance. No, I have no wish to play cards either."

"Harry, if you think I am going to allow you to wallow in the blue-devils, you are very wide of the mark," he murmured mildly. "Try another one."

Reluctantly she picked up the volume and opened it again, scanning through the sonnets. "Now, here's one with more truth in it. 'Tis about lovers who lie to each other."

"I don't want to hear that one. Try One Hundred and Two."

" '*My love is strengthened, though more weak in seeming*'? No, I don't like that either. I think I prefer '*Then hate me when thou wilt; if ever now; Now while the world is bent my deeds to cross—*' "

"Harry, I don't hate you. Quite the contrary, in fact."

She flung the book to the floor and rose to pace before the window. " 'Tis still snowing," she noted suddenly.

"Remember when I was snowed in at Rowe's Hill after Christmas?"

"I try not to think of Rowe's Hill at all. I have not even answered Hannah's letters."

"We made a snow fort, as I recall."

He'd come up behind her and placed a hand on her shoulder. And the strong masculine feel of his fingers rubbing along the bony ridge of her shoulder was almost more than she could bear. Despite her lingering anger and despair, she could not in truth say she was indifferent to his touch. A tremor of weakness coursed through her and she pulled away.

"I think I should like to go outside after all.

Perhaps a walk in the fresh snow will be invigorating. I tire of but sitting, reading, and cards."

"I'll ring for your cloak."

He watched her move restlessly about the room
with some satisfaction. She was slowly, ever so
slowly, regaining the strength that grief and
laudanum had taken, and he had not missed her
response to him in that brief moment.

Taking the heavy cape from Thomas, he draped
it around her shoulders, allowing his fingers to
linger, and then he fastened it, dropping his hands
to brush lightly over her breasts before he stepped
back. He was rewarded by her sharp intake of
breath. Turning away again, she drew on her gloves.

"Ready?"

She looked down at her shoes. "My feet will
freeze."

"Thomas, ask Millie to send down my lady's
boots. And, no, my dear, I do not discourage easily,"
he murmured, reaching to pull the hood up over her
cropped brown curls.

"I can dress myself."

"I know, but it pleases me to do it."

As soon as Thomas returned with the boots,
Richard dropped down on one knee and grasped her
slender ankle. "Lift your foot."

"This is ridiculous. Really, I . . ." But he had her
slipper already off, and his fingers once again
massaged, this time rubbing along her instep to the
ball of her foot. "That tickles—don't."

"I was straightening your stocking."

"And if you do not unhand my foot, I shall be
tempted to kick you with it."

"That I should like to see—you'd land in a heap,
you know."

"Just give me the shoe and be done with it."

Ignoring her, he managed to slip the sturdy

walking boot on and fasten it over her instep. "Give me the other foot, before you take cold from being bundled in the house."

"You know," she complained peevishly, "you are given to queer starts lately. 'Tis as though you do not think I can take care of myself in the least."

"Did you never think I like taking care of you?"

"No." She pulled her foot away after he'd finished with the second boot. "I am not a child, you know."

"I know. Here, help your gallant knight up, will you?"

"Alas, but I will not." A brief mischievous smile brightened her face. "I am for the snow, you know."

With that, she slipped past him and was gone. Her reward was a snowball that sailed past her ear before she'd scarce cleared the steps. Looking back, she could see him bending over to make another from the soft snow that drifted on the porch. Another struck her, powdering the front of her cloak.

"Now, that was unfair! 'Twas a sneak attack! Not even Boney's troops would have been so ungallant!"

"You were used to have a fair aim yourself!" he called back. "Remember when you blackened my eye?"

"And was roundly birched for it!"

The third snowball caught her arm, and the shower of wet snow sprayed upward to her face. "Richard Standen, have you lost your senses?" she fumed.

"There's none to birch you now!"

"No, there's not, is there?" Jumping out of the path of yet another one, she reached down and grasped a full hand of the cold snow, molding it with her gloved fingers. Straightening up, she let it fly, missing him narrowly.

"Come on, Harry, you can do better than that!"

he taunted, running toward her, his arm raised to throw again.

Instinctively she dodged and ran, zigzagging across the snowy lawn. Her breath coming in clouds of steam, she took refuge behind a tree whilst she made her second snowball. Taking careful aim as he moved closer, she managed to hit him squarely on the sleeve.

"Now, are we done with this nonsense?"

His answer came in the form of a solid hit to her middle. " 'Twas most unfair! You have grown bigger than I!"

"Three chances! I'll give you three chances to hit me before I throw again!" he offered, shouting across the open expanse of yard. "But I get to run!"

She looked down at her snow-caked cape and nodded. "I mean to take four, you wretch!"

Millie had stopped on the first landing and watched from the window. "Well, I never seen the like!"

O'Neal, who'd followed her down, peered over her shoulder. "Well, now, 'tis as fine a sight as one could wish t' see, don't ye think, Millie me girl?"

"Shameless! The two of 'em is runnin' like they was the infantry! And her a-peltin' him with snowballs yet!"

"I don't know—Millie, have ye ever thrown one yerself?"

"Not since I was a wee one."

O'Neal's blue eyes took on an unholy light. "Well, you saucy baggage, when the work's done, I'll stand you meself."

"What? Sean O'Neal, I take leave t' tell you I am an honest female!" But there was something in those Irish eyes that set her heart to beating wildly. "I'll be down at three o'clock—the mistress rests then."

"And I'll be a-waitin'. Oh, and whilst ye're downstairs, me girl, have Cook heat some o' that wine punch, will ye? By the looks o' things, his honor's goin' t' need it."

Outside, Harriet was breathless from running, but satisfied with the results. Richard's coat was as snow-covered as her cape. Her hood had long since fallen back from her head, and soft powdery snow dusted her hair, while her face glowed rosy from her exertion.

"Cry surrender, Harry?" he asked softly, walking toward her.

There had been a sudden change in his manner, one that sent shivers that had nothing to do with the cold through her. His dark hair was rumpled from the chill wind and his face was ruddy, making his blue eyes seem more intent than ever. And she was reminded yet again that he was the handsomest man she'd ever seen. Instinctively she backed away.

"No."

He smiled crookedly. " 'Tis as I remember, Harry."

Despite the cold, her body felt hot. "I cannot go back to then, Richard," she managed through suddenly dry lips.

"Aye, you can."

She cast about wildly as he came closer, seeking something to relieve the building tension between them. And bending low, she scooped a handful of the snow and held it behind her.

"Harry . . ."

"Then you must remember this." When he reached the place where his steamy breath mingled with hers, she lifted her hand and dropped the snow down his neck.

"Dash it! 'Tis not quite what I had in mind!"

But as he shook the cold wetness from beneath

his shirt, she turned and ran back toward the house. Panting, she stopped, and from the safety of the doorway she called back, "Alas, your selective memory!" Then, giggling, she stumbled into the foyer.

There Thomas met her with a perfectly straight face, asking, "Would your ladyship have some hot punch? I believe 'twas ordered."

"Let me get out of these wet things first."

She was flushed and breathless, but the thought of hot punch and a blazing fire was tempting. Finally she slipped out of her cloak and mittens and handed them to the footman. "I have dry shoes in the library."

"I'll bring the punch there then."

Richard came through the door stamping his feet to dislodge the packed snow. Grinning, he looked past Thomas to her. "Now, that was most unfair, Harry, and well you know it."

"There's punch, sir," Thomas murmured helpfully.

Richard followed her into the library and divested himself of both his coats and his shoes. Padding noiselessly across the carpet to the fire, he chafed his hands.

"It has been a long time since we've done that, hasn't it?"

"Yes." She'd dropped into a fireside chair and was removing her boots. "And I can do this myself, thank you."

"You enjoyed yourself—admit it."

"Yes, I did, but that does not . . ."

She looked up, realizing that he'd come to stand over her, and her heart caught in her throat. With an effort, she forced herself to remember that this was the man who'd left her.

"I want the old Harry back, you know," he murmured softly.

The inflection in his voice sent another wave of excitement through her traitorous body. Ducking beneath him and standing, she walked instead to the window and stared out into the winter scene again.

"No. You threw the old Harry away, and I think she died, Richard."

"Harry—"

She spun around, forcing herself to anger. "Do you think you can just come back? Do you think I can forget the pain? I loved you beyond everything, Richard, and you left me! Aye, and I've not even the child to show for the love I bore you!"

"Do you want to know why I left? Would it help you forgive? God knows, there's not much I can say to excuse myself, but—"

"No!"

"I left because I felt betrayed, Harry," he continued anyway, ignoring her outburst. "I think I'd come to love you even then, and to think you would scoop so low as to mislead me into marriage, well, I could not bear it."

"Lead you into marriage! Richard, I did not want to wed you, for I loved you too much! Can you not understand? I did not think I could bear to live as wife to a man who loved me not! But then I thought . . ." She floundered for a moment, then collected herself. "I thought perhaps 'twas not hopeless." Her voice lowered, dropping almost to a whisper. "If you felt betrayed, Richard, surely you must understand how 'tis for me. Naught can bring back what I felt for you then."

"I want to live again as husband to you, Harry. I want—"

"You want! Well, I do not!" Backing away as though distance could make it easier to explain, she spoke from the doorway. "Think you I could stand the pain again? No, I should die next time."

"Harry, I'm sorry, and I . . ."

But she'd fled even as he spoke.

The exhilaration of the snowball fight gone now, he sank into the chair and stared morosely into the fire. He'd known 'twould not be easy, he supposed, but it was a new turnup for him. He, Richard Standen, Corinthian, buck of the *ton*, accomplished flirt, and out-and-outer—he lacked the address to win his wife. And he felt the loss acutely.

For a long time he sat staring into the fire, sipping the hot spiced wine. Well, he had not played his last cards. Thus far, he'd been able to force her to go on with living in some small measure. He'd been able to force her to respond even if that response was not the one he wished. No, the battle was far from over, and he still thought it could somehow be won. But not at Richlands. Not where she'd fled when he left. Not where she'd borne their tiny stillborn son. Not where the days were short and gray and cold.

Perhaps if they were far away in another place, another clime, she would again turn to him. Perhaps if they were together as they had been that first week, they could rekindle the love they'd lost.

It was already December, and London would be too thin of company for anything, not to mention that the climate was no more salubrious than that at Richlands. He'd thought about taking her to Italy earlier, and the more he thought of it now, the more the notion appealed to him. They'd see the ancient ruins, drive along the sunny seacoast, and be far away from any reminders of what had passed. And come spring, he'd bring her back to London, take her to the best modistes, and see she enjoyed all the routs and balls she'd missed.

And then he thought of Two Harry. He'd scarce been able to even look at the colt since the accident, and he knew he'd never race him again. But Two Harry deserved the chance to run in the 2,000 Guineas in the spring—it would be a travesty if he did not. Well, someone else could race him, someone who'd not lost a wife and a son.

His mind made up, he walked slowly upstairs, passing Millie on the steps. "Is she all right?"

"Aye. I gave her some of the wine."

"Millie, I'd have you begin packing her things, for I mean to take her to Italy."

The little maid's face fell. "And will I be goin' wi' her, milord?"

"Yes, of course. She relies on you and Alice."

"Oh, thank ye, sir!" Her spirits restored on the instant, she fairly skipped the rest of the way downstairs.

"Flirtin' with the baggage, were ye now, yer honor?" O'Neal teased as Richard cleared the landing.

"Of course not. I told her we were going to Italy."

"Oh. And beggin' yer honor's honor, but ye'll be takin' Millie wi' ye, won't ye?"

"O'Neal, I'll not countenance flirting with the maid," Richard reminded him.

"Flirtin', is it?" The valet feigned hurt. "Now, Millie's a saucy baggage, don't ye know, but there's not a drop of harm in 'er." His irrepressible Irish smile played at the corners of his mouth, making it impossible to maintain the air of injury. "And who's t' say me intentions are not honorable, faith, and I ask ye? Italy now, is it? A fine place for a courtin'."

"We leave right after Christmas. For now, I am going to London to sell Two Harry."

"Sell the horse?" O'Neal was aghast. "But . . . but, your honor, the horse was winnin'!" he sputtered.

"He'll win for someone else then."

21 Her spirits made more blue-deviled by Richard's sudden and unexplained absence, Harriet was even testier than usual. It wasn't right, she fumed to herself. She'd wished him at Jericho, and yet when he'd gone, she was inexplicably lonely. The peace and quiet she'd demanded were hers, but they were totally unsatisfactory.

And Millie's incessant packing and repacking were unnerving. She did not want to go to Italy in the first place, but to have the maid take such ridiculous pleasure in the trip was outside of enough. Even O'Neal, who'd told everybody that the racing circuit abroad had been a dull, lonely business, seemed eager to return to Italy.

"What are you doing now?" Harriet demanded peevishly, disturbed by the sound of crackling tissue.

"Foldin' yer best dress, mum."

"Well, I wish you would not."

"Aye, mum."

"Millie, do you never get out-of-reason cross?" Harriet sighed. "You must surely have the patience of a saint to put up with me."

"Oh, no, mum! Me as knows what ye've been through and all that, well, I know ye don't mean it, anyways."

She began refolding the dress, trying hard not to make as much noise. "Ye know, I like this one the best, mum—becomes ye, it does."

"Thank you."

"It must be grand fer ye to have his lordship a-orderin' things fer ye now. I mean, what with yer not havin' so much when ye was a wee girl and all. Aside from the white dress with the pink sash, that is."

"Who told you of that one?" Harriet asked curiously, laying aside her book. "I'd completely forgotten it."

"Well, when ye was so sick and all—when the doctor told his lordship ye was goin' t' die—well, his lordship was a-talkin' t' ye, a-rememberin' things, ye know." She finished the gown and lifted it carefully to place it with others in the packing trunk. "Made me weep, he did, and Creighton too."

"Oh."

The maid cast a sidewise glance at her mistress and saw she had her attention. Bustling about to take another gown from the wardrobe, she added slyly, "It was when he met ye, he said, that you was a-wearin' the dress. Yer papa was marryin' that Hannah—Lady Rowe, I 'spect I should say—anyways, he was telling ye how ye told 'im ye didn't mind bein' relation to him, but ye sure didn't want that Hannah."

Harriet closed her eyes, recalling vividly now that day. Richard had been handsome even then, and she'd instantly liked his smile. And his dark curling hair. And those brilliant blue eyes. They'd been friends almost from the start.

"But I never knew ye were one for pranks—ye don't seem like it now—'ceptin' for the snow fight, I guess," Millie rambled on, watching her mistress out of the corner of her eye. "I'd not think ye the kind of female child as would ruin yer gown a-crossin' no ford."

"It was on a dare," Harriet recalled faintly. "He spoke of that?"

"Spoke of a lot of things—talked for hours, I think. And when he was done, me and Creighton was a-crying our eyes out, don't ye know. Just wished ye could've heard 'im."

"So do I." Harriet stared absently again, recalling how she'd dared to cross the swirling waters of the swollen ford behind Richard, and how she'd slipped on the mossy rocks, only to be pulled to safety by him. "Er . . . what else did he say?" she asked, trying to sound casual.

"Hmmm? Oh, too much to remember, I daresay. 'Bout how ye was nearly killed by a bull, the both of ye."

"I tried to warn him," Harriet remembered, smiling. "And it was not so bad as I let him think. I would've climbed to safety had he not come back for me."

"But he came back, didn't he?"

"Yes."

"Seems t' me that he was always a-savin' ye."

"After he got me into the scrapes in the first place. He was always wanting me to try things that little girls weren't supposed to do. Once, I fell into the river trying to save my fishing pole. I had to tell Hannah I'd tripped on a tree root, for she'd have never let me go fishing."

"Aye, he was a-sayin' ye were always gettin' punished fer it, and he felt real terrible about that, ye know."

"But we had fun—such great fun, Millie. And he always tried to soften things with Hannah, taking all the blame. But she never listened—it was always my fault in her eyes. 'The Standens,' she said, 'know how to go on as they ought.' "

"He said she took yer spirit."

"I suppose she did." Harriet sighed, still recalling all the birchings. "It became easier to let her have her way, especially when Papa never took my side."

"Well, that part of yer life's done, mum. Ye don't never have t' give 'er a thought again, ye know," Millie said soothingly. "Yer got yerself a husband that loves ye—said so even—but yer was too nigh dead t' hear 'im, I expect."

"He said he loved me?" Harriet echoed almost inaudibly. "No, I never heard."

Millie busied herself folding yet another gown. " 'Tis a pity, for men don't say such that often, don't ye know? And fer him t' have been a-cryin' and sayin' it, 'twas a shame ye weren't awake." She stopped and brushed at an errant tear that trickled down her cheek. "Makes me weep e'en now to remember it, it does."

"Yes, well, I daresay 'twas his guilt speaking," Harriet decided.

"Humph! Ye wasn't there, ye know," Millie sniffed. "Oh, I was prepared to mislike his lordship, and I admit it, but I didn't know 'im fer the kind man he is."

"Kind?" Harriet started to refute it, to remind the girl that he'd deserted her, but then she recalled all the times he'd come to her rescue, all the times he'd been her only friend. The fact that, hating cats, he'd taken three for her. The fact that he'd taken her to the race. The fact that he'd wed her in the first place. "Yes, I suppose he is," she admitted slowly.

"And 'twasn't as though he knew ye loved 'im,

was it?" Millie persisted, now openly watching her mistress.

"No. No, it wasn't."

"Well, I know how 'tis fer ye, fer I've not let on to Mr. O'Neal that I've thrown my hat over the wind-mill fer 'im, neither."

Harriet sat stock-still, uncertain as to which revelation shocked her more. "You think you are in love with Sean O'Neal?"

"Oh, I know I ain't what a man like him'd be lookin' for, what wi' his handsome face and all, but, aye, I am."

"Oh, dear." Her heart went out to the girl, for she knew just how it was to dream of someone above one's touch. "Er . . . you do not think Mr. O'Neal knows?"

"Can't say. Oh, he's kind enough to me—we was a-playin' in the snow like ye and his lordship t'other day, but he ain't said anything to raise m' hopes, ye understand. For an Irishman, he's been a gentle-man."

On reflection, it was quite easy to see how the little maid could be infatuated with Richard's valet, Harriet supposed. He was, after all, handsome in much the same way Richard was—dark hair, blue eyes, winning smile. But he was also a flirt, a man who had a ready grin for every woman in the house, including herself. No, he was not entirely like Richard, for Richard never embarrassed her by teasing the maids.

"Yes, well . . . perhaps you ought to put it to the touch."

"Eh?"

"Perhaps you ought to tell him how you feel."

"Oh, no! I couldn't! Fer one thing, what if he didn't have a care for me? Now I can have me dreams of 'im, but if he was t' spurn me, I couldn't e'en do that."

"Oh, Millie, we must surely be the most miserable of females," Harriet murmured.

"Eh? Oh, no—ye mustn't think that, mum. Ye've got his lordship ferever, and I'm a-goin' t' get Mr. O'Neal. I just go to have me patience."

"Do you have an idea from Mr. O'Neal as to when my husband returns?" Harriet asked suddenly.

"He did not tell me."

Harriet waited until she heard movement in Richard's bedchamber, and then she went to see O'Neal. She found him doing much as Millie had been employed in her chamber: he was packing Richard's things for the trip to Italy. She slipped in the door and closed it behind her, prompting him to turn around and lift an eyebrow.

"What I am going to do is highly improper, but . . ." She stopped, aware his eyebrow had risen even higher, and then she colored, realizing what she'd said. "That is, well, 'tis not what I meant to say precisely. I meant I wished to speak with you as a person rather than a . . ."

"An Irishman, ma'am?" he asked, his smile returning.

"As a valet," she finished. "And I would speak frankly, if you do not mind." Clearing her throat, she found herself suddenly reluctant to broach the matters that had seemed so clear but minutes before. "Mr. O'Neal, you were with Richard abroad—last summer, I mean—and . . ."

"I was with his honor clear 'cross France and Germany and down t' Sicily in Italy," he acknowledged, wondering where she was leading him.

"Do you know why he came home?" she blurted out. "I mean, were the races over?"

A slow smile of understanding spread across his

handsome face. "We could've run Two Harry another few weeks, and Cates was wanting to, but his honor wanted to come home to you."

"You do not have to lie to me, Mr. O'Neal."

His blue eyes met hers, sobering. "Lady Sherborne, there's the time for blarney, and there's the time t' stifle it, and O'Neal knows the difference." He exhaled slowly as though to gain time to phrase his words carefully. "Bein' his honor's man, travelin' fer months with him, I listened to him, don't ye know? And in the beginning, he was angered wi' ye, but the further we went, the more he was makin' excuses fer ye. Faith, and by the time we was in Sicily, he'd made up his mind 'twas yer mama-in-law's fault. And then he wanted t' come home t' ye. We was goin' t' Rowe's Hill t' get ye, but th' shock o' seein' ye here—well, 'twas too much fer him."

"He was coming to Rowe's Hill for me? You are certain?"

"Stopped and bought ye a present at Dover, he did, but wi' the accident, his honor most probably forgot it."

Richard had truly been coming for her. Her heart beat wildly and her spirits soared. And if what Millie had said was true, he loved her. "Mr. O'Neal, did he say when he would return?"

"As soon as he completes the sale of Two Harry."

"*What*?" Stunned, she leaned against the bedpost, clasping it. "But *why*?"

"He couldn't bear the lookin' at it—not after it threw ye. He thought the horse'd nearly killed you." This time, when his eyes met hers, they accused her. "More's the shame on ye, yer ladyship, for ye not to know that. The man'd cut off his arm t' help ye, don't ye know? But 'tis a shame t' sell a winnin' horse," he added mournfully.

"Thank you, O'Neal. Thank you," she responded sincerely. "But we cannot let him sell Two Harry, can we?"

"Well, I don't know how t' stop 'im. I argued the matter with his honor till we was both breathless. ' 'Tis up to someone else to race Two Harry,' he says t' me."

"I'm going to London."

"Are ye now? Then I'm goin' wi' ye, fer ye've got no business on the road without a man—and I'd be there t' see his honor's face when he sees ye."

"It shan't take me long to pack," she promised, starting for the door.

"Well, as we was speakin' as persons, yer lady-ship, 'tis my turn to ask of ye."

"What?"

"Yer Millie—d'ye think she'd take an Irishman?"

"Mr. O'Neal, you have but to ask!"

He watched her go, thinking the trip to Italy would be a pleasant one all round.

22 It was late by the time the carriage drew up in front of Standen House, so much so that Harriet despaired of finding her husband at home. She'd rehearsed her speech a hundred times in her mind, planning what she would say to him, and now it appeared she'd have to wait. She was so absorbed in her own thoughts that she scarce noted the fond gazes that passed between O'Neal and Millie.

"Do you think he will have gone to one of his clubs?" she asked anxiously. "I knew we should not have eaten at that inn."

"Here now, yer ladyship—'tis angered his honor'd be if we was to bring ye all the way here without feedin' ye, wouldn't he? No, 'tis early yet fer the city—his honor don't go till at least eight. And who's t' say he don't mean to be home, anyways?"

As the carriage pulled into the drive at the side of the house to disgorge its passengers, Richard came out the door. And, standing beneath the yellow glow of the gaslight, he looked like the Corinthian he was. His black hair brushed into a rather wavy Brutus, his snowy cravat perfectly tied, his evening coat smoothed over his perfect shoulders as only Weston could do it, he stood for a moment staring as she stepped down.

"Harry! What the devil . . . ?"

"You have not sold Two Harry yet, have you?" she demanded without preamble.

"I am sorting the offers still."

"You did not ask me if I wished to sell my half, did you?"

Incredibly, she was smiling as he'd not seen her smile since he'd come back. His eyes traveled over her approvingly. "Harry, did you come to make me an offer?"

"Yes. But I cannot stand out here in the cold waiting to be asked in, you know. O'Neal, you will see to the bags, if you please, as I do not see a footman just now."

The Irishman looked up, catching Richard's still-stunned expression, and winked, bringing an understanding smile.

"I thought you would wish to be rid of the horse, my dear."

She stepped past him and pushed open the door. "Alas, you thought incorrectly then. How much is the best offer?"

"Ten thousand pounds, but I think I can do better still. Harry, you did not come all this way to stop me from selling Two Harry, did you?"

"Not entirely. Richard, is there someplace where we may be private?"

A wicked gleam sprang to his eyes and his smile broadened. "My dear, I can think of one for certain."

"I should like to settle Two Harry first, I think."

"Then by all means let it be the front saloon—there's a fire already laid in it." He reached to open the door and stood back to let her pass. "Ten thousand pounds is a deuced lot of money, my dear."

"Fiddle. If you sent me but half his winnings, he

should be worth much more than that." She turned to remove her pelisse, bonnet, and gloves, laying them on a small table. Her heart pounded and her speeches deserted her as he shut the door and moved closer. "I . . . I'd like to buy your half, Richard."

"Harry, he threw you! He cost you the child!"

"Yes, but it wasn't his fault, Richard—it wasn't his fault! I . . . I . . ." She looked up, meeting his eyes briefly, then looked away. "He did not want to jump the hedgerow, and—God forgive me—I made him jump. All these weeks that I have punished you, I . . . I have punished myself also. The fault was mine, Richard." A hard lump formed in her throat, threatening her composure. "Two Harry did not want to jump," she repeated in a whisper.

"Harry . . . Harry . . ." His arms closed around her, drawing her close.

"Can you forgive me? Can you?" she sobbed against his chest.

"Can you forgive me?" he countered softly as he swayed back and forth, rocking her. "Can we begin again?"

"You have not answered me," she choked. "I'm telling you that I lost your child."

"And I grieve for him, Harry—believe me, I do—but I grieve more for you. If anything should happen to you, I could not go on." He lifted her chin with his knuckle, searching her face. "Fool that I am, can you still love me?" he asked, his voice suddenly quite husky.

"Oh, yes!" And then, with the perverse nature of woman, she wanted more. She wanted to hear once more what Millie had said. "But have you not forgotten something yourself?" she asked, leaning back against his arm and smiling through her tears.

"Ah, the declaration. All right, Harriet Standen, light of my existence, source of my joys and sorrows—"

"Richard!"

"Harry, you silly goose!" he murmured fondly, lifting her and swinging her around in his arms. "Of course I love you! You have well and fairly caught me! I am the happiest of men! What else would you have me say? That I shall worship you until I die? I shan't, you know, but I'm willing to say it if 'twill make you happy."

"Really, Richard—"

"Oh, that does not mean I shall not love you forever, Harry, for I shall. But do not be expecting me to dote on you from afar, for I mean to be right there with you every day of our life together. We shall live in each other's pockets, and—"

"Richard, 'tis unfashionable, and—"

"You don't wish me to live in your pocket?" he asked, setting her down.

"Of course I do—I shall like it excessively." Her arms crept up to clasp his neck and pull his head down. "But I want you to make no promises you will come to regret."

" 'Love is not love which alters when it alteration finds,' or so the bard said, as you will recall." His face was but inches from hers, so close he could feel her breath against his cheek. "But there have been too many words between us, I think," he added softly, leaning closer to touch her lips with his.

The hurt and the bitterness melted in the heat of a single kiss. She clung to him, her hands clutching his shoulders, as the nearly forgotten fire surged between them, igniting a passion that left her breathless. And when he finally released her, she had to hold on to his arm for support.

"When we get back from Italy, Harry, I'm going

to buy you the finest gowns to be had, and we'll take in every rout and masquerade, every glittering ball, until you are dizzy from it."

"You will not regret you did not get an Incomparable?" she asked, trying not to giggle.

"Harry, I've got an Original—anyone can find an Incomparable, but only I shall have you. I shall have the only viscountess named Harry in the world."

He kissed her again, a long, searching kiss, blotting out everything but the nearness of him. As his hands moved over her body, she felt again the thrill of being touched by him. And with the last tiny bit of rational thought, she managed to whisper against the warmth of his skin, "Will you mind very much if I should prefer to take my horse to Newmarket?" Then, feeling his body go taut, she slid her arm up his back again, holding him close. "I'd rather race than dance any day, I think."

"The 2,000 Guineas?" he murmured, reaching around her to unhook her gown. "If you register your half, I scarce see how my half can refuse to go."